I0575731

Book Prir - Prophecy Transformed

Anna Pattison

Dedicated

to The Lady, Vanadis

Contents

Books In The Norse Prophecy Series   VII

1. Chapter One   1

2. Chapter Two   7

3. Chapter Three   15

4. Chapter Four   33

5. Chapter Five   39

6. Chapter Six   47

7. Chapter Seven   61

8. Chapter Eight   71

9. Chapter Nine   79

10. Chapter Ten   85

11. Chapter Eleven   93

12. Chapter Twelve   103

13. Chapter Thirteen   117

14. Chapter Fourteen   127

15. Chapter Fifteen   131

16. Chapter Sixteen   137

17. Chapter Seventeen   145

18. Chapter Eighteen   155

19. Chapter Nineteen   161

20. Chapter Twenty   167

21. Chapter Twenty-One   173

22. Chapter Twenty-Two   183

23. Chapter Twenty-Three   187

24. Chapter Twenty-Four   193

Map   204

Map   205

"When Freyja and Sven couple
and children are born
then we will trade with many
and our village will prosper."

BOOKS IN THE NORSE PROPHECY SERIES

Book Ein – Prophecy of Love

Book Tveir – The Prophecy Unravels

Book Prir – Prophecy Transformed

ANNA PATTISON

CHAPTER ONE

E ach morning the ice on the well got a little bit thicker. In the chill of the morning, Freyja shivered as she broke it up, and was glad they had stored up much firewood. Tahir had Freyja and Brigit chop even more using the farm axes to work on their war techniques and though they worked up a sweat, their wrists no longer ached. They were nearer their goal of becoming shield-maidens.

Tahir made a rough sledge this morning and they used the horse to pull it to the neighboring farm. The family there waved when they saw Tahir's dark braids and happily welcomed the visiting Moor for he had brought love to their friend and neighbor, Arndis, mother of Freyja.

The twin girls' father was looking to trade his abundant hay. Arndis hoped it would help them overwinter the cows and goats successfully. They brought cheese and fermented roots with them, as well as squirrel and rabbit pelts. Tahir also insisted in bringing the last of his dried fruits left from his trading when he had returned in the summer from Hedeby. It turned out well as the girl's father was happy to add some mead to the trade because of the "exotic" fruits.

The neighbors were starting their preparations for Winter Nights, which marked the end of summer and start of winter. As always, there would be three days of celebration and the *Vetrnaetr Blot* sacrifice. The rumor was that Og would sacrifice a horse in thanks for a good season and they had put aside their best ale for the *Sumbel*, the ceremonial drinking to the gods and elves. They were planning to go to the village on the next full moon. "We hope to see you all there. We will share a drinking horn with you to ensure a good season," the mother said as she hugged Arndis goodbye.

"We will be there. Tahir is getting too used to our feasts and I hope to surprise him," laughed Arndis. "Hail the gods! We are indeed looking forward to even more prosperity." She looked at her daughter Freyja with a proud smile and then quickly at Brigit with a melancholy smile.

Brigit had lived at their farm for almost a year as a captive of a raid on The Far Isle. She and Freyja had discovered that they each wore a half penny around their neck. Freyja's on a leather thong and Brigit's on a silver chain. In talking with Arndis they found that they both had the same father, Brion, who had also been a captive of the village some eighteen years earlier. When his clan paid his ransom, he was returned to Ireland and Arndis found she was pregnant. Brigit had been born of his marriage to another woman meant to ensure a bond of prosperity with another clan.

Arndis shook her head remembering all these details of the girl who had become a valued member of their family and would be taken when they sent for a negotiator for her own ransom. There were mixed feelings in her heart.

Today they all, including Brigit, loaded their backs with hay and piled the sledge high. Without Nora and Gunnar's help they needed to made the same trip for the next two days to bring enough hay back to the farm for their winter needs. The barn loft was stuffed full when they finished and made Arndis smile as she wiped the sweat from her brow. "This is well. I hope to have enough keep this calf through the winter. I do not fear for the milk cow as she is most precious to us." Tahir looked at her and made a face as if he did not understand. "If we cannot feed them both through winter the calf might be slaughtered sooner than I am hoping," said Arndis.

"I am not used to such harsh winters. Always we could find some grass for the animals," replied Tahir.

The days were getting shorter and colder. It was harder to leave the fire after chores and *dagmal*. Dreams were often shared and Arndis would interpret them as long as Tahir would let her. Often, he had to insist that the girls go out to train. "Your god *Thor* will love to test you in all kinds of weather. Better you be prepared. Now let us out to train," he shouted with good humor. He threw his heavy cloak around his shoulders and stomped his feet, clapping his hands. There was nothing to do, but oblige him.

After many days of good training, Gunnar appeared with Nora at *nattmal*. Nora had come with Brigit last year as her maid servant. Upon their arrival she had fallen quickly in love with Gunner. The two spent as much time together as they could either in the village or on the farm of Arndis.

Gunnar explained he was going with a hunting party and would wait for the men to join him here tomorrow morning. "We hunt for meats for our bellies and furs for trade," Gunnar shared. "But tonight, you shall have our company!"

Freyja rolled her eyes, "This means Brigit and I will sleep warm by the fire tonight."

"Yes, at least you will have one night of warmth. I will bring you along to hunt as part of your training," replied Gunnar.

Freyja's jaw dropped, "Do you mean that I should join the hunting party of men?"

"Well, your goddess is a huntress of men," he winked at Freyja. "The Old One has said that, 'the *Seidhkona* sends you to the woods in winter to learn from the blood of the hunt'. I was to say it exactly so," Gunnar added seriously. "Perhaps it has something to do with the *Blot* of the Winter Nights? I do not question the Old One, seeress that she is."

Freyja shook her head, "Nor do I... but, oh well, I can only see what comes of this. Brigit, let us gather furs for our bed."

Brigit and Freyja took a fur each from the bed that Nora and Gunnar would use that night. Nora hugged them, "Thank you for being happy to sleep by the cooking fire," she whispered to them.

"Happy?" Freyja responded with a smirk. "Have we a choice? No, Nora gets her man to keep her warm tonight and we will by the fire lie," Freyja said with a playful frown.

"Do not listen to her Nora, we are all happy to see you. We have missed your stories and help with the chores," Brigit spoke up with a warm smile.

"And have you not missed me?" Gunnar asked.

"We have missed your help with training and with drinking," roared Tahir. "I tire of being a lone man among these women. With these influences I may well become a *seidman* against my will. They would teach me to interpret dreams and other magic."

"Then I have truly saved you, Tahir. Join me in toasting to the night and to the good hunting in the morning," Gunnar smiled as he produced a skin of mead.

The men tossed the skin back and forth until Arndis intercepted it. "The law of the farm is that we share," she interrupted their drinking and took a long swig before passing it to Freyja. She in turn passed it to Brigit, then she on to Nora.

Tahir laughed, "You see, I am at their mercy."

"You are indeed lucky that they keep a good meal fire and feed you well. It makes for a good night's sleep," Gunnar said with a big yawn and stretch. He put his arm around Nora and pulled her up to stand. "Oh, Freyja I am to tell you to get the three spears of your grandfather for the hunt."

"There are spears?" Freyja looked at Arndis. "Mother, do you know of this?"

5

"I knew only of the weapons under the floor. What more of the spears do you know Gunnar and who said this?" Arndis looked to the man wrapped around Nora.

"The brothers of the forge have said this. You will find them in the loft of the barn. The blades are marked with the rune of *Odin* that they made themselves," said Gunnar as he walked with Nora to bed. "Just do not throw them over the head of your prey as *Odin* did over the warriors. We do not want to start a war as in the saga but with the animals," he laughed over his shoulder.

"Well, I will ask *Odin* to help me find them under the hay," sighed Freyja putting her hands on the top of her head. "I will search at first light. So, you all to bed so that I may sleep," she said while shooing Arndis and Tahir toward their bed. She lay down in her fur by the fire and closed her eyes.

"I will bank the fire and soak some barley for the morning while you sleep," Brigit spoke with the exaggerated tone of a servant.

"As you should," laughed Freyja with her eyes still closed. "And thank you, I do look forward to porridge in the morning. Make a big pot, we may have guests. I think that my hunting departure also calls for butter..., lots of it," she smiled and licked her lips.

Chapter Two

Freyja felt a prod to her feet, still wrapped in the fur. She pulled her knees up to her chest, away from the offending kick. "Up. The sun is up and so should you be," Brigit kicked her again. "You need to prepare for the hunt in the wild."

"Not the WILD hunt, but a winter's hunt," Freyja corrected her, uncovering her head. "I will not be prey for ghosts. Thankfully it is not yet Yule," Freyja continued as she sat up, still wrapped in her fur. "Perhaps we will get an elk or bear to add to the *blot* for Winter Nights. The feast would be great then! I should look for those spears to help the hunt." Freyja jumped up, remembering the news Gunnar had brought her of the three spears in the loft of the barn. She hurried out the door.

The cow and calf greeted her with soft lowing. The goat kids ran up to her for head scratches. She gave all the animals some hay to move them out of the way a bit. She held back on giving them oats. It was just the beginning of winter and they may have a long way to go. She grabbed two logs with notches cut in them and leaned them against the loft. Making her way up the stairs she looked into the mass of hay. There was nothing to do, but take it on whole heartedly. She dove in with eyes closed and found her way to the left wall. Feeling her way, she got to the corner. She turned the corner and felt something unusual with her hand. There was a missing upright slat. She put her hand inside to find several mouse nests and then a wooden staff. Then three wooden staffs. She slowly rolled them out and toward herself. She rolled the staffs against the wall as she retraced her steps. Every few turns of the staffs gave some resistance and made a clunking sound. When her foot reached the edge, she slipped. Wavering, still blind, she felt her way down to the floor of the loft and lay on her belly. She could feel her feet over the edge so she managed to force the spears down beside her body and then turn herself around. When her face was over the edge of the loft she breathed deeply and surveyed the scene below. She had disturbed much of the hay and the animals were complaining loudly about being buried.

As she hung her face over the edge she wondered about her next move. Just then Brigit entered and stopped mid-stride. "What is happening here?" Brigit asked. "You poor animals. Come." Brigit opened the door wide and coaxed the goats out and then the cows. She could not see any chickens. Brigit looked around and finally noticed Freyja's face hanging over the edge of the loft and collapsed in laughter. "You are strange, Freyja. Where are your spears?"

"I have found them and they are by my side. May I hand them down to you?" Freyja asked. Brigit nodded yes, so

Freyja began to slide them one at a time over the edge. The first two were staff first so Brigit had no trouble grasping them and taking them down. The third was blade first and Brigit could not grasp it right away so it fell, blade first, into her foot.

"Oh *Eir*, I am wounded," Brigit screamed loudly. Freyja turned herself around and felt for the logs with her feet. She climbed down quickly to lift up Brigit as Brigit held the spear.

Outside the barn, Freyja put her arm in Brigit's mouth. Brigit's eyes locked with hers and she nodded. Brigit bit down hard as Freyja pulled out the spear. They both screamed.

Freyja dropped the bloody spear, picked Brigit up, and ran into the house. Nora stopped her work at the meal fire when she saw them and had Brigit sit on the floor with her foot up on a stool. Nora staunched the blood with her apron. "It is a good clean wound. I will make a poultice and bind it. What made this?" asked Nora.

"My grandfather's spear. I found the three in the loft," answered Freyja with a worried frown.

"Well, I found one with my foot," said Brigit while wincing.

"What is happening?" yelled Arndis coming in the door. "The animals all roam about and I heard screaming." Nora pointed to Brigit's foot. "That explains the screams. Why are the animals set loose?"

Brigit spoke while breathing hard, "When I went to the barn much hay had fallen, from the loft, on to the animals. I let them out while I helped Freyja with the spears. We have much hay to move back to the loft. I think some chickens are buried."

"Well, we will save the chickens and put the hay back in the loft after we know you are well," said Arndis.

"I will help as soon as Nora binds my foot," said Brigit. Everyone looked at her and shook their heads, no. "Then, I will tend the meal fire and then prepare *dagmal* later."

"That will be well. I must to the barn to find the chickens and the spears. They may need to be sharpened and readied for the hunt," said Freyja walking to the door.

"I know that one of them is sharp," yelled Brigit as Freyja left with Arndis, Tahir, and Gunnar following. They all laughed at her joke and Nora took advantage of this distraction to apply the poultice to Brigit's foot. "Ow, this stings my foot," Brigit howled.

"That means it is working," said Nora as she bound the wound tightly. "You will rest here and do no walking," ordered Nora with narrowed eyes. "I will help with the hay in the loft." She added some wood to the fire and put Brigit's foot down on a pile of fur. She patted Brigit's foot unconsciously which brought tears to the girl's eyes.

The chickens were all over the garden, enjoying the last of the spinach and celery. They were busy scratching the bugs they could find under the light frost. The cow and calf had joined them finding some weeds and competing for greens.

Freyja emerged from the cloud of hay dust, coughing, to meet Nora. "They could use help with the last. Much of what we put in the loft fell when I climbed down to help Brigit. I am going to clean these spear tips. They look strong, but will need to be sharpened."

"I will like to see them when you finish," said Nora over her shoulder as she approached the cloud of dust coming out of the barn doorway. She stepped into the barn and greeted the others, "I can lessen your work. I am here to help." The barn grew noisy as Nora joined the others in putting it back in order.

Freyja got a whetstone and drew a bucket of water from the well. She sat on a log to look at the spears of her grandfather.

The wooden staffs were firm and worn smooth. She tested them against her knee and they did not crack or bend. The spear tip that had found Brigit's foot was bloodied, but as she washed it, she found the rune of *Odin* on one side. The symbol, *Ansuz*, had been stamped into the metal and she traced it with her finger. How many times, she wondered, had it found its mark in battle or the hunt? She had heard the tales of her grandfather's bravery and imagined that the chips in the blade had come from a fierce conflict with men or prey.

After some work, Freyja stood the three sharpened spears against the well to admire them. Arndis stopped to look as she approached the house.

"I must have seen these before, though I do not remember clearly." She peered at the rune for *Odin* and wondered aloud, "Not *Freyja's* kittens? Better to have the leader of the *Aesir* on your side. More help is good." Arndis smiled. "Your grandfather is happy that you found these and honor him with their use." She hugged her daughter tightly then turned toward the house, wiping her eyes.

Freyja thought about the mark of *Odin* and felt that she should call upon the god to consecrate these weapons. She hefted the spears and walked to her meadow. She leaned them carefully against a tree and built a small fire. As the fire started, she went to her altar. There she found her carved stone along with Brigit's. She brushed away needles and dirt, then took her stone to the fire.

"In *Odin's* name I light this flame. Cleanse and bless this place." She leaned over the smoke and bathed herself in it. She stood tall, with arms raised. "I call upon you *Odin* to accept me as I wield these spears in your name. Protect me and urge me on in battle and the hunt." Freyja cut her palm with the tip of one spear and dipped her forefinger in her own blood. She traced the *Ansuz* symbol, with the blood on her finger, on each spear then held them over the smoke of the fire.

"I dedicate my spears to you, *Odin*. May my use of them please you," Freyja spoke. She sat on the ground before the fire with the spears on her lap. She closed her eyes. Soon she felt a presence, but it was not the warm enveloping feeling she felt when calling upon the goddess *Freyja*. It was an energizing, urgent feeling prompting her to jump to her feet. "I will honor you, *Odin*."

Freyja stirred then covered her fire with the frosty earth and walked back to the farm. She felt empowered and ready.

Gunnar and Tahir were just entering the house with full buckets of milk and there were eggs on the ground. "I am impressed," said Freyja with a smirk. "You have done well to earn your *dagmal*." She put her spears against the wall and gathered the eggs in her arms. She followed the men into the house.

"Women," announced Freyja. "These men have certainly earned their keep this day."

"Yes," said Arndis. "They volunteered when I wanted to check on Brigit. Nora is busy making porridge and you will get your butter."

"I am hungry and look forward to whatever the day holds as longs as there is butter." Freyja smiled and sat on the floor near Brigit's foot. "I have consecrated my spears to *Odin*," she whispered to Brigit.

"I would say that the blood of my foot was certainly a *blot* to your god," Brigit winked at Freyja. Her laughter was light-hearted and held no malice.

"I am sorry for your pain," frowned Freyja. "You are the first of us to suffer a battle wound." She nudged Brigit with her elbow. "Now you will heal so that we can train more when I am back from the hunt."

Nora was handing out bowls of the barley porridge and then the butter. It was good to have the warm meal on this cold morning and everyone quieted while they ate. Gunnar broke the silence.

"The hunting party is late. We will have little time to hunt today, but may be able to set up camp. Tahir, I will take the sledge in hopes that we get an elk or bear. Freyja, you will

13

need to think on what you can carry as we walk through rough country with not enough snow to use our skis," said Gunnar. "Nora, my sweet, thank you for baking bread. We will want to each take one." Nora nodded with a sweet smile to him and continued to pat out the rounds of dough to place on the flat hot stones near the fire.

CHAPTER THREE

By mid-day the hunters had arrived. They had been slowed by the contributions and well wishes of many. The brothers of the forge sent a whetstone to Freyja, Olaf's wife sent hardboiled eggs with him, and Og had sent squirrel skin hats for all. "Og sends wishes for a good hunt. He is in hopes that more meat may be added to Winter Nights. His wish is that this year we may truly celebrate for three days," said Olaf as he passed out the hats.

Freyja put her brown bear skin around her and belted it around her waist and secured her boots. She had her grandfather's dagger and sword on her belt and his axe in hand. She planned on using one spear as a walking staff and would put the other two on the sledge.

Nora came out with bread. "Here, put these inside your shirts. They will keep you warm for a while." She gave each of the hunters two flat loaves. "Good fortune to you," she said as she hugged Gunnar a bit too long. He finally pulled himself loose and led the others into the woods.

Olaf pulled the sledge behind him while his two friends followed Gunnar. Freyja waved goodbye to all and hurried after them. "I have so many questions, Olaf. I hope you will teach me of the hunt," Freyja blurted out coming along side of Olaf. Olaf only grunted, with a nod.

They worked their way into the woods. Without snow it was hard maneuvering the sledge through the trees, but Freyja helped Olaf tip the sledge here and there. They came upon a clearing after several hours, and with the shortening days, it seemed a good place to set up camp as it was near sunset.

"Freyja, gather wood, while I start a fire. We will need much as the moon is only a sliver, but waxing. Each night we will have a bit more light from *Mani*," said Gunnar. Freyja went back into the woods and cut many of the dead branches that had hindered the sledge. She piled armful after armful while Gunnar built a good fire. After a bit, Olaf's two friends found her piles and carried what she had cut.

"I am Kali and that is my brother, Joarr," said a tall slim man with a short white beard. Joarr nodded in greeting, then his eyes darted around the woods. He was a stocky man who could hold much firewood in his arms. The three of them took the wood to the growing pile and then sat to warm themselves.

"I am glad of the bread Nora gave us," said Kali as he pulled a loaf from his shirt. He bit off a piece and chewed thoughtfully. Olaf had made himself comfortable against a rock and was sharpening his axe. Freyja took his example to heart and tended to the blade of her axe. Joarr stood on one foot and then the other until Kali yelled at him, "In the name of the gods, be still."

"I am feeling something in these woods and it is not good. I will tend the fire this night and keep a close watch," insisted Joarr.

"As you wish," yawned Gunnar. "I will sleep like a baby having done a day's work before our first meal," said Gunnar shaking his head. He proceeded to tell the men of Freyja's adventure in finding the spears of her grandfather and the wounding of Brigit all before they had eaten *dagmal* that morning.

"Brigit is your sister, is she not?" asked Olaf.

"Yes. I told her that I have dedicated my spears to *Odin* and she said that her blood was a good *blot,*" said Freyja. "She does not understand our ways well, but I believe *Odin* took her blood as a good omen."

"I hope for good omens for this hunt" interrupted Joarr nervously.

Again, his brother yelled at him. "If you must jump around, you could be of use and gather more wood or find something to eat. I do not understand what you are doing," said Kali. Joarr left the fire and sprinted into the woods. Kali shook his head, muttered under his breath, then spoke aloud, "He thinks often on signs and omens. I say, just live. Fate will guide our lives. I can only hope to be welcomed to *Valhalla.*" Kali stretched his legs out straight and put his hands behind his head.

Gunnar, Freyja, Olaf, and Kali sat near the fire as the light faded. They sharpened their blades and tended the fire. "I have seen no tracks of game on our way here. Perhaps we will find some fresh in the morning," said Gunnar. They all nodded and saw to spreading their skins out to make sleeping places.

Just as Freyja's eyes felt heavy enough to close, Joarr ran to the fire with wide eyes. "I feel the land spirits of this forest are not happy we are here." He had gathered wild celery and mushrooms and dumped them near the fire. Freyja sat up and took some of each to nibble on.

Freyja spoke with a full mouth, "We must make sure the *landvaettir* are honored. Let us make them an offering." Freyja stood and found a flat rock. She placed some celery and mushrooms on it and a piece of bread. She placed it under a tree and knelt with a hand on the earth. "Hail to the land spirits. We make a small offering to you. We mean no harm to you or your land. Only to take meat home to our hearths." Freyja stood and made her way back to her furs. "This will help. Now you may rest, Joarr," Freyja spoke softly as she touched his arm in passing. Joarr sat by the fire and his shoulders seemed to ease.

Joarr tended the fire and stood watch for the night. He showed signs of great tiredness at first light. The others noted this when they gathered near the fire. His brother, Kali, spoke first, "By the gods, you look awful Joarr. Have you not even rested a bit?"

"I walked most of the night to add wood to the fire and to look for the sounds I heard. I do not feel well," responded Joarr with a worried look.

"Perhaps a *dagmal* will help. I will look for some squirrels or such to go with your mushrooms," offered Olaf. "The rest

of you may hunt as you wish or prepare for today's hunt."
He strung his bow and walked into the woods.

Olaf was back shortly with a squirrel for each of them.
They skinned them and put them on roasting sticks which
they held over the fire. "I am feeling better," said Freyja to
Joarr. "This day will now go well. We have *Sol's* blessing with
a beautiful sunrise."

"I do not know. I feel the need to offer *blot* to *Odin* and
will stay behind today while you hunt," said Joarr hesitantly.
He looked from face to face for approval.

"As you wish," said his brother, Kali, with a disgusted
look.

"You may guard our camp so that we may leave our furs
and the sledge. Make a spit for the fire, in case we bring
back meat," directed Olaf. "Gunnar, Kali, Freyja, are you
ready for the hunt?"

They all stood with eager faces and gathered their
weapons. There was but a little frost on the ground and
Freyja knew that she would heat up with activity so left her
fur at the fire as Olaf had suggested. She noticed that the
others did as well.

They fanned out, all heading in the same southward
direction. There were elk tracks here and there, but each
time one motioned to the others, the tracks led nowhere
as they followed them together. The day wore on in the
same manner. Freyja grabbed wild celery when she saw it
and chewed on it to slacken her thirst. The rough terrain
was a workout with constant ducking under branches and
twisting between boulders.

At mid-day Gunnar took note of the landmarks. "We will go back toward the stand of trees there," he pointed. They all nodded their understanding and went their separate ways toward the same goal.

Freyja came upon a small spring and stopped to take a long drink and fill her skin. She felt eyes watching her and called out, "Hail to the *landvaettir* of this place. I thank you for this water and for the food of your forest. We ask that you give us your blessings on our hunt which will help us celebrate Winter Nights and bring us a good season." She cut her finger with her dagger and caught drops of blood on a leaf to lay by the spring. She reached into the mud and made a patch for her finger before she walked on in silence.

When she reached the stand of trees the others were waiting. Gunnar chastised her, "Why have you kept us waiting? We were ready to go on without you." He glowered at her with just a little bit of worry in his face.

"I found a spring," said Freyja handing her skin to Gunnar. He accepted it gratefully and passed it on. "I made a *blot* to the *landvaettir* at the spring. I will tell Joarr to calm his spirit."

"Did you find signs of game?" asked Olaf. "I came upon nothing. It is strange. I hunted these woods as a boy and always we would have a kill each day."

"I found nothing, as well," Gunnar spoke. "I too hunted these woods long ago. My father had to make us kill only what we could carry that day, there was so much game."

Kali shook his head glumly. "It may be that Joarr brings his fear to the animals. They run away from our camp."

Freyja did not believe that this was possible, but said nothing. As they walked to the camp she went behind and gathered what greens and mushrooms she could find and stuffed them in her sleeves. She even found a berry bush with a few late berries left. She heard Kali call out to his brother.

"Hail the camp! We return from our walk," Kali yelled sarcastically. Joarr stood up from the fire. He had built a great spit next to it, ready to roast a boar or elk. Kali saw it and held up his hands to show they were empty. "We have had no luck this day. I will eat my bread from Nora for *nattmal.*"

"I have brought more mushrooms and greens and even some berries," Freyja said happily as she laid them on a boulder to share. Joarr shot a worried look at Freyja. "I made a *blot* to the *landvaettir.*" She showed her bloody and muddy finger to Joarr to give him the proof.

Joaar whispered to Freyja, "I have made a *blot* to *Odin* this day for our safety in the hunt." He showed her a cut in his palm that he had wrapped with leaves.

"It is well. I have dedicated the spears of my grandfather to *Odin*, as did he. *Odin* should protect us and perhaps tell the gods of our desire for a good hunt," Freyja smiled at Joarr. She hoped that his fears would be lessened.

As the sun set, they gathered around the good fire to eat their bread and forest gatherings. "Bilberries! Freyja, was

21

there more? Did you see animal sign at the bushes? These are favorites of the bear," asked Olaf.

"There were bear tracks about, but they were old. I saw no new sign of any animal in all my walking," answered Freyja.

All eyes went to Joarr, though no words were spoken.

As the light faded Joarr continued to feed the fire. He had gathered more sticks to add to the now huge pile of wood. They settled to sleep in their furs and watched the moon rise, silver bright. The waxing moon now gave enough light to see the way to the forest edge. Freyja often looked to see if there were curious eyes of animals watching, but saw none before she fell asleep.

Many times, in the night, Freyja heard Joarr call out and thrash about in his sleep. At least he was sleeping some. In the morning, he was the last to wake.

Kali came to the morning fire calling all to share the last of his bread. "I have a good feeling about today's hunt," he said. "Joarr, wake up," Kali kicked his brother who slowly sat up. "You slept. See, all is well and you will hunt with us this day."

Joarr sat up slowly and unwrapped his fur. "I dreamt of *Odin*. He has his ravens watching us. There are also hounds nearby. He told me to sleep so I did. Yes, I will hunt with you today."

"Well, let us go then," yelled Gunnar. "We can leave our good camp to come back to tonight." He put out the fire and strapped on his weapons. "Today we head west."

"I agree," said Olaf. "West it is, my brothers!" He laughed when he looked at Freyja and added, "And sister."

Freyja smiled and felt glad she was able to experience her first hunt. The day had begun.

They set off at a fast pace and soon found elk tracks. They followed them down a ravine to a small creek. They lost the tracks, but were able to fill their water skins. Olaf reached into the stream and threw a trout on the bank. He did this four more times so that each had a trout to eat. They cleaned and ate them raw then climbed up the other side of the ravine. At the ridge line they could see a bull elk guarding his herd of cows and calves in a nearby meadow.

They planned their approach and tested the wind. As they got closer a cow moved away from the herd and wandered perfectly inside their circle. The cow turned her side to Freyja and presented the perfect target for her spear. Freyja's hands began to sweat and thoughts of doubt crept in. She said a quick prayer to *Odin* in thanks and froze.

Olaf growled and sent an arrow, but the cow had turned and the time was over. Freyja threw her spear in haste and it went wildly over the cow. The cow bolted back toward the herd. Freyja felt her face redden and clenched her teeth. She ran to her spear then ran after the cow that had joined the herd. The herd saw her approach and turned to run. She was soon left behind until the bull turned to charge her. She did not know what to do until she heard Gunnar yelling, "Run, to the downed tree." She looked over her shoulder to see a large downed tree and ran to shelter behind it. The bull elk charged at Freyja then lowered his head and pushed at the tree. His rack shredded the bark up off the tree and then it rained down all around her. The tree moved with his efforts and she moved back with it. Once she peeked over the trunk just as the bull's rack grazed the top. She ducked quickly, counting herself lucky.

Olaf ran close to the bull and loosed several more arrows, but missed the moving target. He swore an oath and the bull turned on him. Gunnar ran up along the other side of the bull with his spear and the bull put on some speed to leave them all behind. He caught up with his herd and led them south.

Gunnar and Olaf ran to Freyja behind the log. "Freyja," they yelled in unison.

Kali walked over laughing so hard he could not stand upright. "Freyja your spear throw started a war with that bull."

Joarr came up last shaking his head in disbelief as Freyja dug her way out from under the bark chips. She found that one foot was trapped under the tree. The four men pushed against the tree and managed to roll it just barely and it rolled back on Freyja's foot. "Owww," she screamed in agony. "I am stuck."

Kali and Joarr each got a strong branch and put it under the tree to lever the tree up and off of Freyja's foot. Olaf and Gunnar pulled her out. When they were successful Joarr leaned against the tree, his face pale and white. He was sweating and panting.

Freyja unwrapped her boot to find her foot beginning to swell and turn blue. "No, this is not the way to hunt." She put her boot back on and wrapped it tightly. "I will go back to camp," Freyja said bravely.

"I will go too," yelled Gunnar and picked up Freyja to put on his back. She started to protest, red faced, then realized that she probably could not manage on her own. "We will walk together," Gunnar added. They started back to camp. Olaf offered to carry Freyja's spears and followed at his own pace.

"Perhaps we may find something to hunt on the way to camp," shouted Kali at the backs of those who left. He and Joarr started looking for tracks immediately.

The way back seemed quick and easy for Freyja except that she was bounced mercilessly on Gunnar's back. She bit her tongue, saying nothing that might seem ungrateful. When Gunnar neared the fire, she slid down to the ground gratefully. She winced as she stood on her injured foot, then sat down quickly. "I will rest my foot so that I will be ready for tomorrow," Freyja said with gritted teeth. She unwrapped her boot and had a rush of pain. She lay back on her side, trying not to vomit. After she rested a bit, she sat up to look at it further. Nothing seemed broken, but certainly badly bruised. She was glad of the coming cold evening and would leave her foot uncovered for the night.

Olaf got to camp and came over to look a Freyja's foot. "This is not good. You cannot hunt if you cannot walk," Olaf said as he chewed on a piece of wild celery. "Not good. Not a good omen. We have not had luck with this hunt. What will the Old One say? What have you learned?"

"Well, I have learned not to anger a bull elk," said Freyja with a sarcastic laugh. "Perhaps I did not ask the right gods for help and have angered other gods in some way, as well," she sighed deeply shaking her head.

"I found something that may help," said Olaf offering a mushroom to Freyja. "It is warrior's mushroom. It will lessen your pain and make you dream. Perhaps you will hear from *Ullr* or *Skadi*. They may give you advice for our hunt or for your life." Olaf put the mushroom in the middle of Freyja's palm and closed her fingers over it.

Freyja knew that her mother and grandparents used the mushroom when they sought guidance or answers from the dream world. She started to nibble on it as the sun was setting. Joarr and Kali had joined the others at the fire and were talking about the day. Kali laughed, "We have had bad luck before with a hunt. We can butcher a hog or cow for Winter's Night celebration. My biggest fear is the Old One. She wanted us to teach Freyja. So far, we have not."

Joarr looked at each face and then at Freyja. "No, not good at all. I feel we should leave. We are not welcome in this place and will not find game. We should leave."

"Joarr, you worry like an old woman. We will hunt tomorrow and bring something home to your table," Gunnar smiled reassuringly at Joarr. "Rest tonight, my friend. All will be well." Gunnar clapped Joarr on the shoulder and went to make his fur bed.

Freyja settled down in her fur nest away from the fire, wanting the cold for her foot. The others settled themselves about, except Joarr who stayed near the fire. Freyja began to feel as she had had much wine to drink. Her foot stopped hurting and she could hear all sounds amplified. She heard Gunnar fart and Kali laugh in his sleep. Olaf was snoring and Joarr cried out in his sleep once again.

Freyja sat up late in the night without knowing why. A breeze was teasing the fire and it died down low. Suddenly the breeze was in the tops of the trees, viciously twisting the upper branches. She heard hounds barking far off and the temperature plummeted. She shivered and then knew why. It was The Wild Hunt; she was sure of it. "Lie down flat everyone, act as if asleep. Do not move. The Wild Hunt has begun. Spirits are about looking for prey." She lay down and covered her face with her furs. She must have drifted off to sleep.

It was still dark and windy when Freyja heard voices and peeked out of her furs. Olaf, Gunnar, and Kali were leaving. "Let Freyja and Joarr sleep. They are each injured, in their way," said Kali. Freyja sighed groggily. She was still in her dreamworld.

A phantasm appeared to her. *Odin* stood above them all with his spear, *Gungnir,* held high. He shook it and the wind and hounds howled together. *Thor* added lightning bolts to the frenzy as spirit hunters gathered. *Odin* nodded and he and *Thor* retired. The spirits began to slowly drift above the trees looking down for victims. Freyja heard more than one human voice cry out in despair.

Freyja's eyes opened again when the sun was high overhead. She sat up, yawned, and stretched. Her bare foot was very purple and very large. She managed to get to her knees and used a stump to stand. She hobbled to the tree line to relieve herself. On her way to the fire, she saw Joarr with his back to the camp. He must have been looking at something. He was leaning against a tree when Freyja limped up behind him. "Good day, Joarr. What do you see?" She could now see that he had each arm around a tree. When he did not respond she came up beside him to see that those trees were holding him up. His eyes were wide with terror, but there was a slight smile on his lips. He was dead.

Freyja's mouth went dry as she searched the landscape for tracks. She saw none and knew she could do nothing for Joarr. She reached a hand out to try to pry his arm from around a tree, but it was stiff and she did not have the leverage to move him from his gruesome posture.

Her whole body shivered as she limped back to the fire. She threw some wood on the fire and went to her furs. She covered her head and began to breath uncontrollably quickly. Her mind raced. What could be the meaning in this hunt and in Joarr's death? The Old One had told Olaf to say, 'the *Seidhkona* sends you to the woods in winter to learn from the blood of the hunt'.

Freyja gulped air and forced herself to slow her breathing. She muttered softly, "The Old One is a trance woman and sent me to learn. Well, winter has begun and I have killed no prey." Her shoulders started to shake and she began to sob.

Her thoughts became foggy and she felt herself falling into sleep again. Soon she heard the snorts of a pig and wondered if the goddess *Freyja* had sent her boar as a sign. She opened one eye to see not a boar, but a sow with two piglets nosing around the camp. Her spear was beside her and she slowly closed her hand around the shaft. With one mighty heave she rolled and loosed the spear to hit its mark. The sow went down quietly and the piglets were not disturbed.

Slowly, Freyja sat up to begin the task of getting the young sow over the fire. She scooted on the ground to the sow and pulled out her knife to clean and butcher it. She stood and limped to carry the pieces she had cut to the fire. When she had speared pieces onto the sharpened spit, she struggled upright and heaved one end of the spit on to the stand over the fire. She planned to move the coals around to help with even roasting of the meat so grabbed a long stick nearby. "Thank you Joarr, for the good job you have done with this spit. This sow will roast well, because of you. We will all honor you for this meal and will drink to you and praise you well when we celebrate your death."

Freyja decided not to feed the sow's entrails to the piglets, but to burn them in the fire as she spread the coals out. The piglets were finding things to eat around the camp and stopped often to rest in the sun. They did not seem bothered with the disappearance of their mother.

When the men returned to the camp empty handed once again, they found Freyja with two piglets sitting in her lap. "Has your goddess sent you these?" asked Olaf.

"Yes, I believe she took pity on us and sent these and the sow at the fire as well," Freyja gestured to the small blaze. "The gods have given to us this day, but they have also taken. Kali, your brother has left *Midgard*." She sadly motioned to where Joarr stood. Kali's mouth fell open and he ran to his brother.

Kali cried out when he saw his brother's face. "And you left him here, like this? You could not help him?"

"I left him for you as I was unable. When I awoke, I found him, such. He had already passed," said Freyja with true sadness.

Kali unwrapped Joarr's arms from the trees and lay him upon the ground. He found that Joarr had been armed with his sword in his hand and was comforted. "He is on his way to *Valhalla*," Kali said to assure himself as he came to sit with the others. "We must take him to his wife and family."

"Yes, we will leave this place in the morning. Eat what has been provided to us and rest. We will not have need of the sledge for our kill, but for what the spirts have taken," said Olaf wistfully. He leaned close to Freyja. "I heard your warning in the night, Freyja. Perhaps Joarr did not."

Kali snorted. "I heard only the mushrooms talking through your voice. You spoke, 'the *Seidhkona* sends you to the woods in winter to learn from the blood of the hunt' over and over again. This hunt was cursed from the start, as Joarr felt. You made it worse and have brought on Joarr's death. Only by the help of your goddess, did she send one of her brother's pets to feed us." He chewed violently on a piece of the sow and spat some gristle into the fire. Kali continued to mutter under his breath. Freyja's face paled and she turned her head quickly toward him upon hearing the word, *"wergeld"* (payment for a life taken) whispered vehemently.

Chapter Four

At sunrise Kali was putting his brother's body on the sledge. They silently ate more of the sow and Gunnar wrapped the rest in the several cloth bags each had brought. Kali was determined that he pull his brother on the sledge, but with Freyja's added weight it was difficult. After a short time of frustration, Gunnar stopped the proceedings. "I will walk to the farm of Arndis and get the horse." He walked quickly away before anyone could argue.

Freyja sat on the sledge with the body of Joarr and could hardly look at Kali. Finally, Olaf took Kali with him to look for game. After a long time, Freyja heard some happy shouts and joking as they walked back into camp. They had each shot a dozen of the black and white birds called plovers and were excited for the simple meal this would provide. They talked about the good shots, the lucky shots, and the almost impossible arrow shots which brought them their bounty. The birds were packed on the sledge along with the living and the dead human riders and two piglets.

Gunnar rode into view and threw a flat round of bread to each of them. "Nora has sent these for hungry hunters," he laughed. "Now, we have the strong horse to help us." The horse walked up to Freyja and nibbled at her hair until she stroked his neck.

"I am well, old friend. I thank you for helping us home," Freyja patted his chest until Gunnar hitched him to the sledge. Gunnar led the horse and Kali and Olaf walked behind. Freyja and Joarr bumped along. At least one of them did not complain.

Arndis ran out to greet them when they got to the farm. She helped Freyja up the stairs and sat her on a bench at the table. Arndis squealed when she found the two piglets inside of Freyja's top and laughed loudly when Freyja told her the story of how they came with her.

Olaf stomped happily up the steps with several of the plover in his hands. He handed them to Arndis. "For your fire. The hunt did not go well. Freyja will tell you the story." He sat near the fire in anticipation of eating.

Nora ran out to embrace Gunnar for a second time this day, she was more than happy to see him. "I will not stay. I will take Joarr to his family," Gunnar spoke quietly to Nora.

Nora went to Kali, softly touching his arm. "Please come to the meal fire for some rabbit stew and bread. I made it when Gunnar said you were on the way."

Kali looked at Joarr's body then nodded at Nora and followed her up the stairs. At the top step, he stopped and looked over his shoulder once more. At the fire he sat quietly, but ate heartily. When he finished eating, he walked to the door with his head down. "I thank you all and for the use of the sledge to get my brother home."

"Kali, please tell Joarr's wife that I am sorry I could not help him. I want you to take the piglets to her to help her family," said Freyja. She knew others who kept pigs in the village and fed them scraps from their tables.

"I thank you. It will be a help for them. This little sow and boar may bring a small drove for the family," said Kali softly without meeting Freyja's eyes. "I will ask the Lawspeaker if this will be enough for *wergeld*." He clenched and unclenched his jaw. "I will also ask of Og that we might begin the celebration of Winter Nights by honoring Joarr. I will send word."

"I take Joarr to his family with Kali now," said Gunnar. He put his arm around Kali's shoulder as they walked down the steps. Kali wrapped the piglets in his fur cloak and put them on the sledge. He patted the horse on the rump and walked along with Gunner and Olaf toward the village.

Freyja could see them leaving out of the open door and felt conflicting emotions. She was sad at Joarr's death and had felt somewhat responsible when Kali had reprimanded her. If only she had been awake when he went to the trees. Perhaps she could have done something? Did Kali really think she should pay *wergeld* and accept responsibility for Joarrr's death? The *Norns* had woven Joarr's fate and it must have been time for him to join the Wild Hunt or others in *Valhalla*. Luckily, he had had his weapon in his hand. As a warrior, she was sure he would prefer *Valhalla* to *Niflheim* or even *Hel's* table.

Now that her focus had changed, Freyja's foot hurt. She had lifted it up on the bench and now began to unwrap her boot. A wave of pain hit her as the pressure from the bindings was released. She swooned and leaned against the table, whispering oaths.

"Oh my," said Arndis as she noticed. "I will make the same poultice Nora made for Brigit's wound. It will relieve the swelling." Arndis bustled about digging through her herbs.

"These women like to make painful poultices. But it may not be as painful since your wound is not open," Brigit spoke up. Her wound had closed and had a healthy scab. She sat opposite of Freyja at the table with her foot up and twisted her body to get a good look. The pair were a sight and Tahir took note of it when he walked in.

"Only if I were drunk, would I choose those two legs! Thank the gods I am not given the same choice as *Skadi!*" Tahir roared. Brigit stared at Tahir with knitted brows.

"Arndis has told me the tale of the giantess, Skadi who had to choose her husband by the sight of his legs alone. The two legs of yours might only be chosen by one who was drunk," laughed Tahir while shaking his head. "Arndis says she would have chosen my legs," grinned Tahir while turning his ankle seductively.

Arndis put down her herbs and came to Tahir. "Yes, your legs remind me of the warm summer earth. Especially when they are wrapped around me." She grabbed Tahir's sleeve and pulled him in for a kiss. "I must be back to my work of poultice making," she patted his butt and went back to her work.

"Yes, work is good. Now to find some work for the two of you, since you cannot train." Tahir rubbed his hands together gleefully. He looked around for a bit. "At the table, you will sharpen all the blades on the farm. We start with the cooking knives." He nodded to Arndis who wiped her knife on her skirt and brought it to the table. "I will bring you whetstones that the old brothers sent to you, Freyja," Tahir yelled over his shoulder.

Tahir brought the stones and Nora and Arndis laid their knives on the table. Soon Tahir brought the farm axes. Nora brought Brigit's axe, sword, and dagger to lean them against the wall. Freyja's weapons had been brought inside from the sledge and were close by already. Brigit and Freyja looked at the growing pile and sighed at the same time. They set to their task as the light from the open door faded and was then shut to keep out the night. They worked more slowly by the firelight. Nora brought a bowl of water and a rag for them to wash the grey from their hands then set the night meal before them. "Now it is time to eat. You can sharpen more tomorrow," Nora said.

Brigit had been sleeping on the floor, near the fire, since her foot had been wounded. Freyja thought it would be easiest on her foot to do the same. Together they looked like two bear cubs nestled in the furs. "Good night sister," whispered Freyja. "I am sorry I wounded you."

"I forgive you, sister. Besides, it seems the gods have seen fit to give you your own foot troubles," giggled Brigit. "I am sorry for your pain, but not sorry to have your company." She reached over to pat the furs covering Freyja. "I had fever dreams while you were gone," Brigit shivered. "I dreamed of wind and dogs howling. Spirits roamed around the outside of the house whispering."

Freyja took her head out of her covers. "What did you do then?"

"I was dreaming. I slept. As I will now." Brigit yawned and snuggled down in her fur.

"It was no dream," insisted Freyja in a lowered voice. "*Thor* made the winds blow fiercely and *Odin* stirred the spirits to The Wild Hunt."

"What is that?" asked Brigit.

"It happens on nights of winter. The hounds howl and the spirits search for souls to join them in their hunt. I saw it on the night of Joarr's death," Freyja sighed heavily. "It is good you stayed in bed. It is best to lie still and quiet so the spirits do not take you forever with them on the ride of *Asgard*."

"So Joarr is with *Thor* and *Odin*? Is this not an honor?" wondered Brigit.

"To be with *Thor* or *Odin* is always an honor, but the spirits of the Wild Hunt know no rest in *Valhalla*. They must always hunt. I fear that is how it will be for Joarr," Freyja said quietly.

CHAPTER FIVE

For days Freyja and Brigit sharpened blades. Sometimes they would take a break to braid each other's hair. Brigit wanted to put in many small braids in Freyja's hair but she cautioned her. "My braids should be simple as is my life. We may put many in your hair as you are from a great house." Brigit seemed to take this in and followed Freyja's instructions.

As the pile of blades dwindled, Nora or Arndis would bring back a kitchen knife or their own women's knives for sharpening again. Tahir found scythes and a plow blade as well. Work on the farm always required a sharp blade.

They finally finished with their own weapons. "Are your blades in need of sharpening?" asked Brigit. Tahir looked around as if not sure she was asking him. Brigit scowled. "Yes, you Tahir. Do your weapons need an edge on them? We have become very good at it."

"You may trust in our skill, Tahir," Freyja insisted. "You have instructed us well and may look for yourself." Freyja waved her hand over the table full of sharpened items.

Tahir came to the table and made sounds as he picked up an axe to test it. "Yes, you do good work. You may start on my blades and then I will take them out in the sunlight to put a fine edge on them myself." He seemed hesitant to give them total control over the condition of his weapons. "A warrior should be responsible for the care of their own weapons," he said by way of explanation as he walked outside.

The next morning, they heard Gunnar's voice singing out, "Nora, my girl. I am here." He left the horse and sledge and ran into the barn when he heard her voice yell back in response. He carried Nora out in his arms, laughing.

"Be careful, I have a pail of milk here," Nora giggled. She wiggled out of his arms while balancing the pail skillfully. "Let me put this down so that I may welcome you properly, Gunnar." She put the pail down and wrapped her arms around him for a passionate kiss.

Arndis and Tahir came to the door to witness the reunion. "You are well met, friend. Turn her loose and I will help you with the horse and sledge," Tahir announced. He walked to Gunnar and gave him a hearty hug. "See, you have been missed by all." Together they unhitched the horse and let him graze while putting the sledge behind the barn. "Come in and tell us all the news."

Nora had brought the goat's milk inside and started the cheese making process. Gunnar came up behind her to wrap his arms around her waist. She laughed and slapped his hands away. Arndis brought him a cup of broth and some bread and Brigit put her foot down and patted the spot next to her on the bench. Gunnar sat with the air of a returning hero. "Tell us the news, Gunnar," Freyja prodded, even though his mouth was full.

"The moon is near full and on the night of full moon we will begin the three days Winter Nights celebration. Og will sacrifice a horse and we will feast at his long house. Joarr's family is building the pyre and we shall send him to *Valhalla* on the first night. The gods will surely attend us," stated Gunnar. He ate more then stopped to look at Freyja. "Kali has asked the Lawspeaker to pass judgement on the death of Joarr. Kali says that you are responsible and he will have reparation of *wergeld* or vengeance."

"He did mutter '*wergeld*' when we left our campsite in the woods, but I was not the cause of the death. His saying so is a mighty insult," Freyja's hand tightened into a fist. "Better he seeks reparation from the gods." Freyja's face was reddening. "I tried to warn you all of the Wild Hunt. Joarr must have been about when the spirits came near."

"I will speak on your behalf because I was at the camp with you during the night. But, Olaf, Kali, and I left while it was still dark in the morning and you and Joarr were sleeping. I know not what happened while we were gone. Only that Joarr was dead when we came back," Gunnar spoke in measured tones as he watched Freyja's face.

"You cannot believe...," Freyja stood up at her bench, her mouth open. She swept her arm across the table, knocking knives on the floor and hobbled out the door. Gunner, lifted his cup of broth just in time, and stared after her.

Brigit started to follow on her own wounded foot, but Arndis put her hands upon her shoulders. "It is well that you leave her alone."

Tears of anger and pain streamed down Freyja's face. The Old One had sent her on the hunt. *Odin* and *Thor* had revealed themselves on their Wild Hunt. She had done nothing, but try to learn, which included her use of the mushroom. Her warning to the others was noble, but she could not tell them what to do. "*Cattle die and kinsmen die.*" She heard a voice plainly and sat down on a stump next to the well to think.

So, everyone dies. Joarr died as was his *wyrd,* his fate. She stood to look down at the still water in the stoney well. Her eyes swam with tears and the surface of the water blurred. She saw a vision of single combat.

Two figures, with shields and swords, were surrounded by a crowd. They each broke two shields in their turn and were tossed a new one when needed. The crowd cheered mightily at their movements. They fought violently until blood appeared on the ground and they were halted. She could not tell which was the victor. She felt pain in her left thigh so strongly that she grabbed it, panting, and sat down heavily on a stump. She rocked back and forth, pressing her hands against her thigh.

What vision was this? Was this a portent of the future? Her eyes were red and swollen and she did not want to climb the steps to the house. She slid down on the cool ground and put her foot on the stump. Freyja closed her eyes as the sun was bright.

Freyja opened her eyes when a shadow fell across her face. Tahir was standing over her, offering her a cup. "Gunnar has brought good mead from the Mead House to share. It will be gone before you make it inside, so I have brought it to you." Freyja accepted his outstretched arm to help her sit up and took the cup in her hands. "It may soothe you," said Tahir softly.

"I thank you, Tahir. My foot hurts, but my mind hurts more. I do not understand how Kali can blame me for the death of his brother," Freyja spoke wearily.

"I do not know your beliefs, but I believe that men are caused to die in many ways. I saw no blood, no wound, on his body and know not how his life was taken. If you say the gods were involved, I believe you," Tahir took her empty cup. He offered her his arm and helped her stand, then helped her up the steps. "No more running on this foot. I want it to heal so we can get back to training. And I tire of doing your chores," Tahir smiled at her.

Freyja sat again on the bench across from Brigit and put her foot up. Her mother came with a new poultice for both girls. Brigit sighed with pleasant relief and Freyja sucked her breath in between her teeth, wincing. Gunnar and Nora had left the fire and Freyja was glad. She did not feel like defending herself.

Tahir wandered to the open door and Arndis followed. He leaned his lanky body against the door frame to watch the rising moon. "The moon is full soon. Gunnar has said to go to the Winters Nights festival at full moon." He pulled Arndis close with his free arm.

"Yes. It is our custom to gather for three days at the start of winter to sacrifice in thanks for a good season and in hopes for the future season. We have only a little frost on the ground so we will have comfort for our stay. We shall drink ale, *sumbel*, in *Odin's* honor. We shall feast on Og's kettle cooked horse and all good foods that people bring. I will bring many cheeses and Nora will bring bread. The neighbor's farm will bring honey, ale, and mead. Such good times we always have," smiled Arndis remembering past gatherings.

Gunnar and Nora came from the barn with milk pails and paused to watch the moon as well. "This year we will also honor Joarr on his way to *Valhalla.* It is good to have us all together and *Mani* will surely guide us. We will leave before moon rise tomorrow with the sledge loaded with our wounded and our provisions," Gunnar spoke as one who knew the routine of local festivals. It was true that he had grown up in the village and knew all the families and the local practices. He and Nora brought the milk inside as Arndis pulled Tahir playfully away from the door.

"Milk for our cheese makers," Nora said with a smile. "It is good to start more as we are taking much with us tomorrow. Let us bless your table with plenty." Nora brought supplies to the table. Brigit and Freyja rolled their eyes, but began the process.

When they finished, Arndis brought them some boiled roots with honey and some of the plover that Olaf had shared with them. Everyone ate and went to their beds. They were eager to wake early and prepare for the festival tomorrow. Everyone, but Freyja. She tossed and turned in her furs, worried about Kali and his ideas of *wergeld*. He wanted payment for the death of Joarr and the Lawspeaker would decide if he was due reparations from Freyja. What payment could she offer? Perhaps their winter store of cheese, roots, and dried meats, but that would make a hard winter for them. They had animals, but again those belonged to more than just her.

The weapons of her grandfather were the only other thing of value that only she owned. She would not part with them willingly. "Lady, *Vanadis*, I ask for your protection and guidance with this challenge," Freyja whispered to her goddess. She closed her eyes and willed herself to sleep.

Freyja woke and found Brigit was still asleep. The meal fire had been built up, but no one was near. She heard the voices of the others outside. There was yelling and laughing. Nora came in with only goat milk. "Wake girls, you make some fresh goat cheese only. The cow is not milking," Nora smiled as she put the goat milk on the table. "Get up and begin your day. You have little to do while the rest of us get ready for our walk to the village celebrations. I am making bread."

Gunnar came in with wood for the fire and Tahir brought in eggs. Arndis had dug some roots through the light dusting of snow on top of the frozen ground. Her pail was full and she was very chatty. "We have gotten the sledge out and each must put their furs on it. I will take these fresh roots and cheese. Nora your bread smells good."

"Eat some, everyone. There is goat milk, bread, and roots from last night. We have much butter as well," Nora was listing items from their bounty. "There is much to do before we leave at moon rise."

"I will take bread with me and check the snares. I put some out yesterday, Freyja. I do not set them as often as you did, but I have kept us in rabbits these last days," Tahir winked at Freyja.

Brigit and Freyja helped each other down the steps to wash at the well. The journey there and back was slow, but they felt refreshed when they settled at the table. The fresh bread and roots tasted good and they set to the next batch of cheese. "We cannot walk to the village. My foot is much better, but I cannot walk that far," Brigit shook her head. "With the frost it will be now easier for the horse to move the sledge. I hope we may ride along."

"My thoughts were those as well. We ride the horse or the sledge. We are not as helpful as we were in the past," Freyja made a sad face. "But we have now sharpened all the blades." Freyja brightened then thought. "Oh, please don't tell Gunnar that we will sharpen his blades." Freyja let her head fall back pretending to faint.

Chapter Six

By sunset the furs had been gathered and loaded on to the sledge with food and cooking pots. Gunnar hitched the horse while Arndis put the goats and chickens away for the night. Tahir helped Freyja and Brigit into the sledge and Nora handed them bundles of bread and herbs. They started toward the village. All were smiling, in a festive mood.

At the fork, on the road to the neighbor's farm, they came upon that family walking. They all had bundles on their backs and hailed the group from Arndis' farm. "Freyja," the twins sang out at the same time. They walked next to Freyja to hear the tale of her injury. Then their mouths gaped when they heard Brigit's story as well. "You are two women with only two feet," laughed one of the twins. They walked together for the journey.

The father spoke to Arndis, "I have a servant going to your farm morning and night as we spoke of. He will tend the animals and feed himself from their bounty." Arndis nodded in thanks knowing that it would make for a more relaxing three days if she did not have to worry about the farm.

The caravan stopped at the Mead House. Many from the village were walking past, toward the shore and the pyre for Joarr. Gunnar unhitched the horse. "The road is too muddy and torn for the sledge," he said. "We will leave it here." He offered Brigit his arm to help her out of the sledge and lifted her onto the horse. Tahir did the same for Freyja so that the girls rode toward the towering flames.

When they got to the edge of the sand the horse stopped and out of nowhere Sven appeared. He reached up for Freyja's waist and lifted her down. She shivered just slightly as her skin tingled. She remembered how it felt to be held by a lover. When Sven set her down their eyes met then he quickly looked down. "Thank you," Freyja said gently and smiled at him as he looked up. Sven nodded then reached up for Brigit. He lifted Brigit down to the sand then took both girls by the arm to steady their walk to a large log. He sat each down and went to sit on the other side of Brigit.

Freyja turned her attention to the scene. The pyre had been well built and the flames had grown large. The smoke had now grown greasy gray with the consumption of the body. Within the edges of the smoke cloud rising in the sky, Freyja clearly saw a group of *Valkyries* with outstretched arms. She looked around to see if any others had seen this. All were chatting quietly while watching the flames. There was one other face searching the crowd. The wrinkled eyes crinkled as she smiled and nodded toward Freyja and then the *Valkyries*. The Old One waved her arm toward the specters and yelled to the crowd, "We send Joarr to *Valhalla*. The *Valkyries* embrace him and take him to sit with *Odin* where the brave may live forever. Hail, Joarr." Voices rose to echo her, "Hail, Joarr.""

Og spoke up, "We will drink to Joarr as we begin our Winter Nights celebration. Join me at my table!" Og took Helga's arm and waved the crowd to follow him up the path and to their farm. The crowd grew louder as they left, having turned from death to feasting. There was laughter and singing.

Most all were leaving except Joarr's family who stayed near the pyre. Brigit leaned toward Freyja to say, "I go on Sven's horse." Freyja watched as Sven lifted her half-sister up and led the horse from the beach toward the festivities. She sighed just a bit, but then decided to enjoy the peace for a while. She turned on the log to face the inlet and enjoy the sound of the waves.

A figure approached her and she recognized it as Kali. He had a drinking horn in one hand and his other was under his tunic. He took a wide stance in front of Freyja and made of show of working his member under the fabric. Freyja looked away. "I will ask for *wergeld* tomorrow," Kali intoned ominously. "The Lawspeaker will hear my case and decide you owe me payment." Kali stepped toward Freyja and pushed her legs open to stand between them. "I have a way that you can pay me without going to the Lawspeaker."

Freyja kicked her good leg up and over Kali's head to bring it to the other side of him. She bent both knees to knock him on the ground. Hobbling up, she stood with a foot on each side of him, her dagger drawn. "I am of more value than twelve *ell* of cloth for a bed slave. I am a free born woman and no man's slave."

Kali pulled down on Freyja's skirts, causing her to lose her balance and go down on her knees. The dagger was knocked from her hands. Kali fumbled with Freyja's skirts, pulling them up around her hips. She put all her energy into her knees and pinched his legs between them, then rolled herself to one side. She found her dagger with one hand and reached for Kali's penis with her other hand. She held the blade against his skin and he froze. He began to whimper. Freyja allowed her blade to barely nick him then rolled to her knees.

Kali stood and brushed himself off as he rearranged his tunic. "I will speak with you and the Lawspeaker tomorrow. You will pay for the death of Joarr and this insult," Kali hissed as he hurried away.

Freyja pulled and draped herself across the log, breathing heavily. She sheathed her dagger and after catching her breath, sat upon the log. This turn of events would complicate Kali's claim. Now she had a claim of insult as well. She would make sure to tell all to the Lawspeaker.

The beach was empty except for the ashes of Joarr. The night was quiet except for the lapping of water against sand. Moonlight no longer revealed any *Valkyrie* and Freyja did not feel Joarr's presence so knew he must have gone on to *Valhalla*. She whistled for her horse who lumbered to her. He allowed himself to be pulled over to the log so she could stand on it to mount him. She leaned forward to hug her oldest friend and was soothed by his warmth. She put her ear to his skin and listened to his heartbeat. She could feel it within her own chest. She sat up and they moved as one, slowly, toward the village.

She stopped in front of the Mead House. "Hail the house," she yelled and one of Halig's slaves came out. It was the olive-skinned woman who spoke very little. She pointed down the road toward the farm of Og, which Freyja took to mean that the people were there for Winter Nights. She motioned for Freyja to stay and turned quickly around to go inside. She came back with a cup of mead and offered it. She looked up shyly with her dark and heavily lashed eyes. Freyja wondered why she had never noticed the beauty of this woman before. "I must look tired and in pain. I thank you for your kindness," Freyja said with a raspy voice. She handed back the cup and the woman held her hand for a long moment, sympathetically.

Freyja let the horse continue at its own slow pace. A few slaves were traveling to and from the celebration, presumably following orders. When she got to the farm, she could hear that the *sumbel*, the ceremonial drinking of ale, had begun. She dismounted and limped into the hall of Og's farm. She found a bench she could sit on as she listened. "Hail the gods. Hail the ancestors. Hail to the *landvaettir* and the *husvaettir*. We ask you to bless our festival and bring a good season to us all," the Old One spoke loudly for one of her age.

"Now, fill your drinking horns. We dedicate these horns to *Odin*, The AllFather, and we drink. Hail *Odin*! Pass your horns to kith and kin and drink to a good season!" Og's speech cheered his assembled guests. Freyja was passed horns by many and drank until her foot stopped hurting. She found bread and meat presented to her as well. She ate enough to fill the hole in her belly, but not in her heart. She made her way outside to the sledge and her furs. She gathered together a warm nest and slept to the sounds of the feast.

The next day showed many fires around which visiting families gathered. Freyja woke to Arndis, Brigit, and Nora at their fire. Tahir and Gunnar were helping on the farm.

At midday a slave girl came to their fire. Freyja recognized her as one of Helga's weavers and a slave by her short hair. "Og calls you to the Lawspeaker, Freyja," she said with obvious excitement. Freyja closed her eyes and grimaced. Kali must have brought the Lawspeaker before Og and spread the news of his claim of *wergeld*.

"We will come with you," Arndis said. She helped Freyja stand and walk into Og's hall. Nora and Brigit followed, which gave Freyja some courage. "There is Kali, across from the Lawspeaker. Joarr's wife is on his right and his own wife is next to her," Arndis whispered. Arndis wanted to tell Nora and Brigit of the people involved.

More people were gathering. The news must be spreading. The whispering grew. Gunnar and Tahir appeared and came to the women. Olaf came and stood by himself.

In time, Og stood and addressed the crowd. "Kali has called for the Lawspeaker. He claims *wergeld* from

Freyja for the death of his brother, Joarr." The whispering intensified. The Lawspeaker stood and all were quiet.

This man was well respected and had trained under many older lawspeakers. He had attended meetings held at the *Thing* gatherings of leaders to study the ways of law in all aspects. It was whispered that he was so knowledgeable he must be descended from the god of law himself, *Forseti*.

He was middle aged with only slightly greying temples in his chestnut brown hair and his brown and grey beard fell to his waist. He wore several silver and gold chains that rested across his beard atop his barrel chest.

He spoke in a deep and resonant tone. "Kali, you say Freyja is responsible for the death of Joarr?" the Lawspeaker asked. Kali nodded, yes. "Do you have witnesses?" Kali motioned for Olaf and Gunnar to come stand before the Lawspeaker.

"How did his death happen?" the Lawspeaker looked into Kali's eyes.

"When I came to the camp, Joarr was dead. Freyja was the only one with him," answered Kali.

"Why were they alone?"

"We left in darkness to hunt. Olaf, Gunnar, and I. Freyja and Joarr stayed behind."

"Why did you leave them behind?"

"Freyja's foot was wounded. Joarr was not well in his mind," offered Kali. Olaf and Gunnar nodded.

"Why do you say he was not well in his mind?"

"Each day he would speak of the land wights not being happy we were there. He felt we were being watched. He spoke of a curse on our hunt. Even when Freyja made offering to the *landvaettir* with him, he was not appeased," Kali spoke ,while Olaf and Gunnar nodded again.

The Lawspeaker searched the crowd and called to Freyja. "Freyja, come. You must be present while claim is made against you." Tahir took Freyja's arm and helped her walk forward. The Lawspeaker looked at her limp and at her foot wrapping. "How was your foot injured?"

"A bull elk turned on me. I hid behind a fallen tree and he pushed so that the tree rolled upon my foot, Lawspeaker," Freyja responded.

"Saw you this?" The Lawspeaker looked at the men and Kali, Olaf, and Gunnar all nodded. "So, you left Freyja at the camp with her injured foot and Joarr because he was mad?" The men all shook their heads, no. "Did he kill himself? Were there wounds or marks upon his body? Who found his body?" All the men looked at Freyja and the Lawspeaker's eyes followed. "Tell me what you saw."

"I woke midday to see Joarr standing, with his back to the camp, at the tree line. I called to him and he said nothing. Perhaps he did not want to disturb game so I came near, slowly, on my wounded foot. He did not turn, so I came to his side and saw his face. He was dead," Freyja explained.

"Did you see marks or wounds? How did he die?" the Lawspeaker prodded.

"I saw no marks. His arms were each around a tree as though he was watching. He carried his sword in one hand." Here the crowd murmured their relief. "His eyes showed surprise and there was a smile upon his lips. I believe he was taken to join the Wild Hunt." The crowd erupted with noise. There were gasps, snorts, and some wild eyes. The Old One made the hammer sign.

The Old One came forward. "Tell me why you believe this," the Old One looked sternly into Freyja's eyes. "What do you know of the Wild Hunt?"

"You have told us all of the nights when spirits hunt. *Odin* and *Thor* may lead the specters as they hunt and those of *Midgard* who are about may be taken along." The Old One nodded and raised her eyebrows, wanting to hear more. "In the darkness of the night I woke to hear the wind howling in the tops of the trees. Hounds were howling all around. I looked to the sky, from my sleeping furs and saw *Odin* and *Thor*. *Odin* motioned the spirits to ride and they rode over us."

"Did any of you others see this?" the Lawspeaker asked the men of the hunting party. Kali and Gunnar shook their head no, but Olaf stepped forward.

"I did not see, but heard the wind and the dogs howling. I also heard Freyja call out that we should lie still and quiet," Olaf spoke seriously. "I know the stories and did not want to be taken."

The Lawspeaker stood tall. "I see nothing that says Freyja killed the man or caused his death. She shall not give you *wergeld*, Kali. Is Joarr's family now under your care? If not, it shall be so."

Kali interrupted, "Freyja's magic caused his death. Perhaps she worked a curse with the land wights or did curse him with her *seidr*?" Kali was obviously still pursuing *wergeld*.

The Old One stared at Kali. "This cannot be as I have not taught her such magic, yet." She smiled broadly at Freyja and patted the seat beside her. Freyja sat down gladly.

"Then, not *wergeld* for Joarr's death, but she insulted me mightily last night. I will ask for reparations."

The Lawspeaker's chin went up as he sat. "Tell me of this insult."

"Last night she has cut my manhood," Kali said the words boldly and dramatically. His wife stepped forward and nodded emphatically.

"This is indeed an insult. What have you to say, Freyja?" The Lawspeaker spoke harshly. "Why did you cut him and in such a place? Are you lovers?" At this Kali's wife looked between Kali and Freyja with a pinched mouth and angry knitted brows.

"No," said Kali quickly. "She attacked me..."

Freyja could be silent no longer. "I cut him when he tried to rape me. There was nothing of love. He said he would not ask for *wergeld* if I would lie with him. When I would not be his bedslave, he tried to rape me."

Kali yelled back. "I did not want a bedslave," he swore to his wife. "I would visit your farm, such as Og used to visit your mother." At this Helga's face reddened and Og held up his hand to stop Kali.

Freyja rose to her feet. "*I* ask for *wergeld* from Kali. *I* have been insulted. He tried to rape me and now he calls me a bedslave, worth no more than ells of cloth. I am a free born woman," Freyja screamed at Kali.

"You may be a free born woman, but I know your family well enough to make such a proposition," replied Kali.

Freyja and Arndis both tensed visibly.

Brigit took a large gulp of air and stepped forward to stand next to Freyja. She lifted her chin and took Freyja's hand in hers. "We are the daughters of Brion, a chieftain of his clan. Freyja is indeed too high-born to give to you."

Everyone stopped talking and looked at each other. They all knew that Brigit and Freyja were half-sisters. The fact that Freyja was also high-born had never been considered. They lived in two different worlds. They could not be compared.

"Another insult," yelled Kali with a red face.

The Lawspeaker walked to the middle of the room. He held both hands high. "I see there are many insults, one against the other. No one has right to atonement unless they avenge themselves. I call for *einvigi,* single combat, as the way for you to settle your grievances. Kali and Freyja looked at each other with stunned anger in their faces.

The Old One interrupted, "Freyja has a wounded foot and cannot yet fight for herself."

"I will avenge myself this day," insisted Kali. "I will fight for my honor and for *wergeld*." He pumped his arms while pacing back and forth.

"I see no honor in fighting a wounded opponent," Tahir stepped forward. His black hair stood out amongst the bleached golden and red hair.

"You are not her family. You cannot be her champion," Kali spat the words.

"I am the man of her mother, Arndis. This makes me family and I will fight for her honor and in her stead. Tell me the rules of this combat and I will honor them."

Freyja walked to Tahir and took his arm. "I thank you for your willingness, but you do not have to do this."

"I am in the hands of the gods. I will do my best." Tahir winked, "It is good that you sharpened my blades." He took his dagger out of its sheath and shaved the hair on his arm.

The people were all talking and milling about now. There were shouts of excitement and people giving directions. The Lawspeaker and Og went outside and the crowd followed. A clear area was forming as the two men gathered their weapons. Each had a sword and shield of his own.

The Lawspeaker stood in the middle of the people. "For insult given and insult received, we begin *einvigi*. Kali claims *wergeld,* as does Freyja, for insults. Kali will fight and, for Freyja, Tahir will fight. Two shields may be given each, from a friend. A mortal wound, as a wound to the thigh, will end the contest. The people make a square for you," he shouted loudly.

The people pulled back to create a square. The Old One stood tall and raised her hands to the north. She made *Thor's* sign of the hammer and spoke loudly. "We ask the god of *einivigi, Ullr,* to attend this duel for *wergeld*. May the honorable prevail."

The crowd grew silent. Kali lunged wildly at Tahir who darted away easily. Tahir was light on his feet and returned a smashing blow. Kali met it with his shield which resulted in a chip on one side. Kali swung his sword blindly away from his body and met only air. Luck was with him as Tahir landed a harsh blow again on Kali's shield which protected him before it shattered.

Olaf called out, "Kali, my shield to you." He tossed his shield to his friend. Kali hefted it above his head for show with a smile for all. His wife and Joarr's wife cheered. Tahir waited while Kali made this show to his friends then stepped forward to land a light blow on Kali's sword arm. Kali pulled it back with a grimace. A thin line of bright red blood showed through his sleeve.

Tahir was a skilled swordsman and was excellent at defense with his shield. He danced away from Kali's sword so long that it was almost comical. Freyja suppressed a giggle. "It is well for me that Tahir is my champion. I hope that he is careful," Freyja worried to her mother. "I fear only that Kali may use some trick to win."

"Do not fear. Tahir has told me tales of his duels. They are common where he is from. He has been the victor many times," Arndis comforted, with her voice as well as her hand on Freyja's.

Tahir swung his sword and Kali dove under so that he rolled on the ground. Kali came up with a handful of dirt. He threw it in Tahir's eyes. Tahir only laughed and spat. He wiped the back of his hand across his eyes and renewed his attack. He stepped to the side of Kali and spun around behind him. Tahir turned and Kali turned. Tahir struck Kali on the thigh. Blood poured from Kali's thigh as he fell to the ground.

"I will pay *wergeld* to Freyja," Kali cried out. He clutched his thigh and motioned to Olaf for help. His wife ran to him and ducked under his other arm to hold him up. Joarr's wife looked angry, but ripped the bottom from her skirt to bind the wound. She clenched her jaw and looked daggers at Freyja when she was done.

The Lawspeaker shouted, holding up one hand. "All will be still." The people quieted. "Kali has ended the *einvigi,* contest, by offering *wergeld* to Freyja. He is also thigh wounded. It is done. What say you, Freyja?"

Arndis helped Freyja stand to speak. "I accept your offer of wergeld for insult, Kali. I do not want your coin in my house, but ask you to give coin or exchange work to Joarr's wife. She is the one who is truly insulted by Kali's actions." She spoke to the Lawspeaker. "Is it well that I ask this?"

"I will speak with Joarr's wife to see that she is given what she is due," the Lawspeaker nodded once. He turned to the crowd and addressed them with a booming voice. "We have interrupted our Winter Nights celebration enough with this *einvigi*. Let us again give *blot* to The AllFather for a good season. Bring your good ale for *sumbel* to *Odin.* Tonight, the feast continues!"

Chapter Seven

There were two more nights of feasting as usual for Winter Nights. Kali and his wife left to their home to heal his wound. Joarr's wife and children stayed at Og's and were well fed and cared for. All honored the man that Joarr had been. His wife wanted to stay on their own farm and many offered help until the widow found a new husband. A wealthy woman would have many choices.

Nora and Gunnar, Tahir and Arndis feasted and spent time at the fire. They all helped at Og's farm with work and with feast preparations. Sven often came to take Brigit around Og's farm, so Freyja spent much time alone with her foot up, tending the fire. She watched the children playing and listened to their laughter. It was good to see the people of the village enjoy themselves, gathering to ensure a good coming season.

With the Winter Night's feast done, Tahir loaded the sledge and the girls rode back to the farm on top of the furs. They brought back empty kettles and bags. The food had been well enjoyed and shared. Tahir's sword and shield were tucked in as well. "We shall need to sharpen the blade of your sword, Tahir. You have nicked it on Kali's shield,"

Freyja said. She held it in the sunlight while Tahir walked along side of the sledge.

Gunnar turned his head around from leading the horse. "You will sharpen his sword? I know nothing of your skills in this." Gunnar looked surprised. Freyja pantomimed biting her tongue to Brigit, which made her start giggling.

"Both girls have sharpened all the blades of the farm. Their skill has increased with Tahir's teaching," Nora spoke. She walked next to Gunnar leisurely, enjoying the sun especially in the cold weather. Her breath came out in clouds as she spoke. The sledge moved smoothly on the light sheets of ice. The horse's hooves broke through the ice on occasion, but he was surefooted and did not chop up the path badly.

When they got to the farm, they found a fire and root stew ready. The neighbors had sent a slave girl to care for the animals each day of Winter Nights festival and she took it upon herself to make a meal. She held the door open for Freyja and Brigit as they limped up the steps. She smiled and pointed to milk pails on the table then ran toward her home.

Brigit sat by the meal fire, and for the first time in a long while did not put her foot up. She unwrapped her boot and Nora came to look at her wound. "It seems the skin is holding. Now you have only a nice scar," Nora smiled as she pulled both sides of the skin. Brigit stiffened her back, but then relaxed. Nora rubbed some saved fat on the skin. "Tomorrow you will do the milking again."

Freyja looked on from the bench at the table with her foot up. "I am sorry I wounded you, but in your own way you gave *blot* to *Odin*. My grandfather put *Odin's* rune on the spears before your foot was pierced. Now the AllFather will watch over you," Freyja smiled at her sister. "Maybe you should have the rune of *Ansuz* on your scar?"

Brigit made a face at Freyja. "And you? Perhaps you need the rune for the elk, *Algiz,* on your foot?" Brigit laughed. Freyja made a face and laughed along.

When Freyja woke the next morning, she was alone by the fire. She hobbled around and found some barley soaking so started some porridge. She found a good amount of honey so put it out as well. Just as the porridge was ready, Arndis came in with goat milk, followed by Brigit. Brigit sat down hard on the bench, "Whew. My foot will need to become strong again. I have been lazy."

"Yes. Only your hands have worked. But you have now walked to and from the barn and done milking. This is good," Freyja encouraged her sister.

"And she will do it again in evening," Arndis added. "Freyja, you have made porridge! This day begins well. I see honey, too. This is how you like it, so we will see how this special day unfolds."

Gunnar came in and took his sword and dagger from his belt to lay on the table in front of Freyja. "I would like to see how you sharpen these." He sat across from Freyja. "I told the Lawspeaker what I know. I do not think that you killed Joarr, but I could only say what I know. I am sorry for Kali's indiscretions. I wish I had been at the pyre to defend you." Gunnar looked down at the table and sighed deeply.

Freyja reached over and touched his arm. "I was angry, but I know you spoke the truth. Thank you for your words. Now, I will show you how well I sharpen your blades. Bring me the whetstone," Freyja said smiling.

Tahir came inside to see Freyja working busily at the table. "I see Gunnar has learned of your talent with the whetstone. I too am in need of your attention to my blade." He took his sword out of its scabbard and laid it on the table. Freyja took a big breath and blew the stray hairs from her eyes.

"Tahir, first I will finish Gunnar's blades and then I will start on yours. I cannot say when." Freyja took her foot off the bench and stretched her neck and sighed. "I will seek the sun for a moment." She stood and limped for the door. Outside she reached the well and drew water to wash her hands and face. She shivered when the cold water hit her face and neck but then laughed. As Arndis said, this may be a special day. Freyja sat a few moments in the rays of the midday sun watching the clouds coming and going. A chill wind came up and snow began to lightly fall. Freyja sighed and felt the call of the warm fire. As she climbed the steps, she heard an approaching horse.

Turning around to look down the path, she saw Sven was walking his horse and a small figure wrapped in furs was riding. The figure carried a distaff as a magical symbol of a *volva* or wand-carrier. The tool for spinning sat atop a long staff denoting a connection to the shaping of destiny. Freyja knew it to be the Old One. "Mother, the Old One comes!" Freyja yelled through the doorway. She immediately heard bustling inside.

"Nora, add to the stew. Brigit, tidy up those furs. Gunnar, take your blades from the table." Arndis shouted orders. She and Tahir hurried past Freyja to greet the Old One as Sven helped her down from his horse. "Come, we have fire and food for you. Welcome. We are honored." Arndis was excited.

The Old One smiled and hugged Arndis firmly. "I come to see Freyja." She waved Freyja to her and took her arm. They walked away from the others. "At Kali's claim for *wergeld* I said I have not taught you many things. I would like to help your teaching as s*pa-kona*." She turned and waved Arndis and Tahir away. "I will come in my time." She looked in Freyja's eyes, "Show me where you do *blot,* or honor the gods. Tell me how you speak with your goddess."

The women walked to Freyja's meadow while Arndis brought Sven inside. Arndis watched the two women from the open door as they walked through the softly falling snow. She loaded Sven's arms with several furs. "You will take these to them," Arndis insisted. She pushed Sven toward the door.

Freyja led the Old One to her altar. The old woman lent surprising strength to Freyja as she limped along. "Here I do my *blots*," explained Freyja. The Old One pointed to the carved rocks and nodded a question. "This is my stone, the black one is Brigit. Long ago I made a stone for Sven, and my stone and Sven's stone stood side by side when I first did *blots* for the prophesy to unfold." Freyja's voice was sad. The Old One seemed impatient and looked around. Freyja led her to her fire and offered the stump to sit on. "I often speak with the goddess Freyja at my fire." The Old One opened her arms. Freyja took her flint out to start the fire. She gathered dry wood and blew the flames to life.

Sven appeared with the furs and placed them quickly beside the Old One. He backed up wordlessly and hurried back to the house. Freyja took one fur to sit upon the ground and placed one around the Old One's shoulders and one across her lap. Freyja spoke to the fire, "Sacred flame, in *Freyja's* name cleanse this place. We also honor the *landvaettir* of this place. Hail *Freyja*. We offer our hearts and thank you for your teachings." The Old One nodded her approval.

"Some *spa-kona* speak with those who have left this world of *Midgard*, do you?" the Old One searched Freyja's face.

"I have heard my grandmother often. She would speak of the mighty passion, *inn matki munr.* She would tell me of the love between she and my grandfather and her hopes for me to find the same. No longer do I hear her. Not since the prophecy changed." Freyja looked dejectedly down at her hands.

The Old One chided her, "The prophecy did not change, only our understanding of it. We learn and we grow. Now you must still find your own way to fulfill the prophecy. This is your path and your responsibility," the Old One instructed sharply.

"Your grandmother was a *spa-kona* and she taught your mother some. Did not your mother speak with your grandfather concerning his weapons?" the Old One asked. "This was an important part of the gods' support of your training as a shield-maiden."

"Yes," replied Freyja. "She used the warrior's mushroom to help her dream my grandfather to her," Freyja answered. "He gave his blessings and she gave me his hidden weapons." Freyja felt better realizing that other people also spoke with those in the next world.

The sun began to set and Freyja and the Old One still sat by the fire. Freyja listened to stories and songs. The Old One banged her staff, with the distaff on top, on the ground as she chanted. Freyja felt tired, then energized by the chanting. She felt cold, then warmed. It was a dizzying time which flew by. A figure appeared near them with warm bowls of fragrant stew which were taken without words. Still the Old One told stories of the gods and their history among their people. "The Norns have woven our fate long ago. We may try to change it, but it will still be as they will. They may change our wyrd and we will adapt. Or not," the Old One laughed and stood. "Come, it is dark," she spoke as if this was a surprise to her and indeed it felt to Freyja as if they had talked only for a few minutes.

The old woman and the young woman hobbled to the steps and up into the warm house. "Welcome," Arndis ran to help the Old One to the bench at the table. Freyja peeled her fur off and helped the Old One do the same. Their faces glowed. "Here is warm mead for you," Arndis put cups on the table. "We have a bed for you." The Old One drank her cup and asked to be shown to the bed.

When Arndis returned, she and all looked at Freyja with wide eyes. Freyja looked very intently at her mead. "Well?" asked Arndis. "You have spoken long with the Old One."

"She has told me stories and will teach me, but she says I know much already. I ... do not know ... She says you will also show me much, Mother," Freyja looked at Arndis then yawned. She felt as if she had eaten a warrior's mushroom or had too much mead. "She said that you and my *amma* are *spa-konas*, too."

"I?" Arndis looked around. "Perhaps your grandmother, but I? I ... do not know ...," Arndis sighed and shook her head. "I know little, but I will show you what I do know. Now, you seem to need sleep. Come to bed with me. Tahir and the others will all keep to the fire." The mother helped her daughter stand and go to the back room. Tahir made a face, but Arndis blew a kiss and smiled at him such, that he could not feel slighted.

Tahir went to the pot to find more mead and filled every cup with the warmed honey liquid. Tahir, Gunnar, Nora, Brigit, and Sven spoke in low tones for a while. Then all set up their furs to sleep, each wondering about the Old One's visit.

At first light Nora was up making bread. Brigit was sent to milk the goats and Sven offered to help. Tahir checked his rabbit snares and returned with two large hares. Arndis let Freyja sleep and made barley porridge. Gunnar put a finishing edge on his blades while waiting for food.

"What goes on?" Freyja asked loudly when she came into the room. All waved their hands and shushed her. "Where is the Old One?" Freyja whispered.

"That is why we ask quiet of you," Arndis whispered fiercely. "The Old One sleeps." She handed Freyja a bowl of porridge. Freyja looked at the honey, but Arndis held up her finger and shook her head, no. "The Old One first, then you may have some."

Moments later, the Old One tottered into the room. She looked younger as if the sleep had made her so. "We are well met," she spoke to the group. Arndis placed a bowl of porridge on the table for her where she seated herself. Arndis offered the honey to her and she waved it off. "Freyja will want it," she said with a wink. She ate with focus on her bowl making sounds of enjoyment. When she finished, she stood and called for Sven, "Sven, come. We will go."

"But we need to know what you wish of us," Freyja stood in front of her. "What should I do now? How shall I learn? How do I now fulfill the prophecy?" Freyja begged.

The Old One stopped and took one of Freyja's hands. She also took one of Sven's hands. "You two are bound together to fulfill the prophecy and must work together to do so. You, Freyja, will be shown how to bring prosperity and you, Sven, will be guided to bring us trade." She put their hands together. Freyja felt the familiar tingle of Sven's skin upon hers, but dropped his hand immediately.

Freyja did not feel like working with Sven for any reason. Sven's eyes went to Brigit while the Old One walked out the door. "I thank you for your hospitality," she said and she climbed up on a stump to wait for the horse. Sven ran to get his horse ready while all came outside for the sendoff.

Freyja hurried to stand beneath the Old One. "How shall I learn? " she implored. "When will you return?"

The Old One looked down and put her hand on Freyja's head. "You must listen and be silent. You must look with eyes open and closed. You must dream while asleep and while awake," The Old One's voice was gentle but firm, "You will see me again, when you need to."

Everyone waved goodbye to the Old One as the horse was led away by Sven. The snow was falling gently and all but Freyja went inside. Freyja stood looking after the Old One and her old lover. She felt like she had been given much information but understood very little.

CHAPTER EIGHT

T he snow continued to fall and, over time, walking to the barn became difficult. Time was spent making skis to help with further travels such as hunting. As the giantess *Skadi* and the god *Ullr*, Freyja and Tahir went to set and check the snares on skis. Freyja's foot had returned to normal size and she was once again doing her part on the farm.

Tahir and Gunnar had the girls out in the snow to practice with spears. There were many targets for this, but the worst part was retrieving the spears which provided good exercise as the drifts grew deeper. Soon sore shoulders and arms became strengthened. Many days they came inside laughing, red faced, and out of breath.

As the shortest day approached, the farm was busy preparing for the celebration of Mid-Winter Night. There would of course be another sacrifice and feasting to ensure this year's good crops. The neighboring twin girls had come by to say the celebration feast would be held at the Mead House. It was more centrally located and Og had given permission. At the market place, people were talking about the new location. Halig had already asked the twin's father to bring as much mead as he could spare, which started tongues wagging.

Nora and Arndis made mittens and boots out of rabbit skins for trade in anticipation of the gathering. It seemed long since the feast of Winter Nights. Indeed, it would be several moons between the two feasts.

Freyja worried that Kali and his wife might still carry ill feelings toward her and Tahir because of the *einvigi*, but she determined to hold her head high. The Lawspeaker had made judgement, on the claims for *wergeld* and the *einvigi*, both in her favor.

Tahir cut and smoothed some staffs that people might want to use for spear making. Brigit and Freyja continued to make cheese from the goat's milk to add to their stores. Gunnar was at a loss for some way to contribute to the industry around him. "I know not what to do with my hands or time these days of snow," he moaned. Nora came to put his arms around her waist. "Yes, my hands are well used on you, Nora," Gunnar laughed and hugged her.

The next day Tahir and Freyja entered shaking snow off their cloaks and boots after checking the snares. Tahir stood his skis against the wall and came to the fire. "Gunnar, the skis you have made work well for me. Because of them we have rabbits now, instead of at sunset," Tahir exclaimed.

Freyja skinned and cleaned the two rabbits. She cut them up for the pot and added water and salt. "Gunnar, I like my skis as well." she said. "I think you should make more. Perhaps they can be traded to those who do not have the skill to make them. I would like you to do some more carvings on mine as well. Then I will not confuse them."

Gunnar smiled. "Now I know what to do with these hands," he held his hands up. "I know where there are logs we cut and that have dried. I will make good use of them." He grinned from ear to ear as Nora patted him on the back.

Many days passed with everyone doing their part on the farm as well as creating items for trade. When the moon was full Tahir brought the sledge in front of the house and asked all to load it with their contributions and sleeping furs. Gunnar hitched the horse to the sledge and all put on their skis. They made a fine scene walking to the Mead House. The path had enough snow packed on top of ice to make pulling the sledge easy for the horse. Nora sang as they traveled.

They were joined by more people as they got closer to the village. People called to each other in greeting and shared wishes for good crops to come. A large fire had been built in front of the Mead House and Og had his slaves butchering several wild boars. "Hail to the house of Arndis," Og yelled as they approached. "I have hunted well and we feast tonight! Welcome." Og came forward to meet them. He smiled as a gracious host and patted all on the back. "Let us have no *einvigi,* but enjoy ourselves," he said in a low voice to Freyja and Tahir. Freyja made a disgusted face at him, but Tahir nodded and smiled.

Gunnar unhitched the horse and cleared some snow from the grass so that he could eat. Both sledge and horse were under some trees so their household might retire there. Gunnar saw Olaf and went to put his arm around his shoulder. They went quickly inside for some drink.

Tahir had the pleasure of joining the women as they found a table and benches inside. Halig, the owner, quickly came to welcome them, "Welcome friends we have many to drink and luckily much drink to share. Freyja, Brigit, will you help with the filling of cups and horns when it is time for drinking to the gods? We will toast to bring good crops."

"Yes," answered Freyja. "I will help for this celebration. Many are here and will be happier with full cups." She smiled at Halig and patted his hand.

"I too, will help," Brigit volunteered. "I have enjoyed the Winter Nights festival and will now know Mid-Winter Night. The people here feast and celebrate well."

"We have many reasons to be thankful and offer *blot* to our gods," Arndis interrupted. "You now will have seen two of our season celebrations. We had *Vetrnœtr* or Winter Nights at the end of harvest and the beginning of winter when we sacrificed in thanks for a good season. Now we celebrate *Jol* or Mid-Winter Night, in the middle of winter, and we sacrifice for good future crops. At the end of winter, we will celebrate *Sumarmál* to welcome Summer Time and sacrifice for victory. You will see them all before we send our ship to bring your ransom and negotiator back." Arndis' voice sounded cheerful until she realized that the talk of the negotiator meant that Brigit would be leaving them. She smiled weakly. "Tonight, we celebrate!" she said a bit too loudly.

Freyja again had mixed emotions at the thought of Brigit leaving, but turned her attention to the gathering. Many were at the back of the Mead House asking for cups to be filled. Freyja took her cup and one more to stand and wait. Halig's slaves were filling cups. The two male slaves spoke and laughed with people, but the dark-haired woman was silent. She took Freyja's cup and smiled at her. She was so different, Freyja thought. Olive-skin, brown eyes, and long dark hair. She had not had her hair cut as all slaves did as a sign of her station. Freyja wondered why. The woman filled Freyja's second cup and held her hand a moment when she returned it. Perhaps that is normal in her culture, Freyja thought, as this had happened the last time the woman offered her a cup. Freyja thanked her and was rewarded with a gorgeous smile. Freyja went back to the table. She offered the cup to Brigit.

The boar was roasted and served late in the night. Cups were raised when the Old One, seated on her high seat, spoke to all. "Hail the gods! We come on Mid-Winter Night to sacrifice to ensure good crops. We thank *Odin* for healthy children and good crops of the past and those to come. Fill your cups and horns to drink to *Odin* and the gods!" the Old One shouted.

As the crowd surged toward the mead Freyja and Brigit hurried to help fill cups as promised. Freyja bumped elbows with the dark-haired slave woman and they worked well together to help all.

"Now," the Old One continued. "Hail to the gods. Drink!" All obeyed then she dipped her cedar brush into a bowl of the boar's blood and made the sign of the hammer over the crowd. The splatter of blood covered many of the celebrants and the crowd roared their approval.

"Hail the gods!" the people yelled together. The merry making continued until sleeping children were carried home and old people escorted out. Only a few of the young stayed to drink further and many couples had found other things to occupy their time. Freyja saw that Tahir and Arndis had left, as well as Nora and Gunnar. Brigit and Sven were sitting at a table talking quietly.

Freyja sat alone until the slave girl joined her. They sat quietly making signs to each other as Freyja did not know if the girl shared their language. When Freyja lifted her cup and said, *"Skal"* the girl responded and lifted her cup. They sat comfortably in silence. Freyja set her furs near the fire to sleep. "Good night," she said to the girl. The girl nodded good night and Freyja watched her climb a ladder to the loft.

The next two nights were much the same, but the days were filled with trading. Gunnar traded his skis and the mittens and boots were well received. The cheeses were eaten at the feasting. Tahir made a deal with the old brothers to share profits from spears that they would make the blade tips for. Tahir would deliver more staffs to the brothers.

At the end of the days of celebration, the group packed their furs and some trade goods on the sledge and headed back to the farm. They had acquired some honey and mead. Sven waved to Brigit as they skied away and Freyja looked back to see a dark-haired figure leaning against the Mead House doorway. The slave girl was a wonder to her and she could not stop thinking about her and how she had come to be in their village.

Once home to the farm all things resumed a routine. The box that Tahir had recently built for the sledge came inside so that Freyja and Brigit had a bed. Tahir and Arndis and Nora and Gunnar continued to share the beds in the other rooms. "This is well to bring the box inside for our bed, Tahir," Freyja said. "I am thankful to be up off of the floor."

"I thank you too," Brigit said. "We now have several more moons until I can see the Summer Time festival. I am anxious to see more of your sacrifices."

Nora smiled at her, "I think you are more anxious to see something else." She clucked her tongue and then laughed.

Time seemed to drag on with milking, trapping, spear work, and crafting. Often Freyja felt the need to be out of the house and away from the others. She would walk to her altar and make a fire to offer *blot* to The Lady. She would leave mead, food, and special flowers or stones that she found as offerings. She tried to follow the Old One's advice and look, listen, and learn. Her heart felt full when she spent time with her goddess and she was comforted. Her path, her *wyrd,* was entwined with the weeper of gold.

Freyja offered her own tears when she felt hopeless or conflicted, but soon she would notice a sign of hope. The goddess encouraged her by leaving hawk feathers in the crotches of trees and guided her to herbs and mushrooms that, at first, seemed hidden.

Chapter Nine

As winter was ending the days remained unremarkable. Freyja felt at peace on the farm at first, but now wanted more than anything to move about the forests more freely. She was hoping for something to change and at the same time was anxious for what that change could be.

Several mornings had now brought the sound of ice breaking along the shore. Loud pops could be heard as sheets of ice shifted and ground against each other. The thaw had begun and the ship would be back into the water soon enough.

Freyja wanted to climb the rocky prominence to check on the preparation of the ship leaving for the Far Isle again. They would be leaving as soon as the ice let go of their ship. They would have the warmer weather to negotiate for Brigit's ransom. After spending the time, to procure a negotiator, the crew would return to the village before the ice would once again lock the ship to their shore. Prosperity in the form of ransom would be welcomed. The promise of treasure would bring prosperity, but Freyja would then be without Brigit. Bitter-sweet surely.

She climbed the rocks to watch the ship and thought of what provisions they might spare to give to the journey. Hopefully they would have put away enough to last through the last bit of winter and to contribute. Though she only saw a few at work, many of the youth she knew would be going on this trip. They would be well supplied by their families, but she felt the gesture would let the people know that she supported the mission. She would remember to ask Arndis what they could share when it was time.

Freyja came into the house thinking about the preparations of the ship. "Mother, will we have something to share with the ship that leaves soon? Perhaps some of these roots?" Freyja asked.

"These today will not be ready for their journey, but we have many under the house floor and will send some," replied Arndis.

"It seems they will leave soon from what I saw from the lookout. I will take our contributions." Freyja added, "Perhaps it will assure them of our goodwill and support. I will begin to gather what we send to the ship. I will use the bag I made by *nalbinding* and put two pots of fermented roots in it," said Freyja. She was perfecting the craft of nalbinding she had learned from the neighbor, the mother of the twin girls, and was proud of her rough, but serviceable accomplishment.

Brigit was interested in the proceedings, "I would like to see the ship preparing. May I come with you?"

Freyja's eyebrows raised. "I did not know how you would feel about this ship and its mission." She had not had a sibling and now understood the feelings of an older sibling protecting a younger one. All three of the women smiled at her, encouraging her to make the magnanimous choice of including Brigit.

"I will get the horse," offered Arndis.

"I have herbs to put in a pouch I made of rabbit skin," added Nora. Brigit stood as if ready to go.

Freyja threw her hands in the air knowing she could say nothing against this, "All right. She comes with me."

Freyja placed the heavy bag on Brigit's shoulder then climbed on the horse while Arndis held its mane. Brigit stood on a stump and Freyja reached down to help the shorter woman up on the horse behind her. "We take the cliff path to the beach and perhaps then go to the Mead House. We may be late," Freyja called over her shoulder as they left for the boat. Arndis and Nora waved happily as the two departed and Freyja imagined that they would be chatting into the evening as their friendship had developed deeply. Her own relationship with Brigit was more than a friendship. She had so many conflicting feelings about her and still not all of them were positive.

They began the steep ride to the beach on the path of switchbacks. Freyja could hear Brigit suck in her breath a few times as she looked down the rocky fjord cliff. It started to annoy her when Brigit grabbed on to her so she took some pleasure in taking a few risks on the narrow path, which only resulted in more grabbing so she relented and slowed down to be more careful. Brigit was obviously aware that Freyja was being more careful as she managed a tense, "Thank you. You were being a bit reckless."

Freyja smiled over her shoulder but still allowed the horse to slowly lumber on to the sand, rocking the women intensely back and forth. Brigit took the opportunity to quickly slide off and knelt gratefully in the sand. She looked up to Freyja and made a face as she got to her feet, then continued to walk beside the horse. Both shielded their eyes from the low sun to look down the beach at the ship.

Freyja's eyes fell on the large log near the ship that had hidden her and Sven from the eyes of several shipmates after the raiding of last season. She imagined that she saw the imprint of two bodies in the sand from love making, then shook the image from her mind. The image left, but not the knot in the pit of her stomach. That meeting with Sven had been an instigation of her passion. When Sven had responded in kind, she believed that their future had begun to unfold according to the prophecy. She had also wondered at the two cloaked figures walking toward the village that Sven had watched after longingly.

Brigit looked at the departing ship and shivered remembering when it had delivered her to the village and to the sister she had not yet known. When she had been carried from the boat, she had clutched her cloak more tightly about her hoping for its protection. Now she smiled as she searched for the tallest blond head she knew would belong to Sven.

There were many gathering to help stock the ship and ready the crew. Kegs of water were being loaded aboard along with various food stuffs. Bread, dried meats, and seaweed, pickled items from many farms, and salted fish were included. The fish could be saved for later as the men would no doubt fish from the boat. The oars were being placed after repair. The men would bring their own weapons and any personal items when they were ready to leave.

Freyja recognized Klause standing near those who would be taking this journey. He had promised the Old One that he would help to guard the village while the ship was gone. (His friend Karle had stayed behind last year.) While Klause had felt it to be an honorable duty to his village and the Old One Karle had been bitterly scornful, having to stay behind. When Klause saw Freyja approaching, he called out. "Hail Freyja, our goddess of prosperity!"

Freyja managed a half smile. She no longer felt the same confidence that had once accompanied her position tied to the prophecy. The half-sister walking beside her was a reminder of her lost legacy and her unsure future yet to unfold. They were all pinning their hopes on this voyage and the ransom that they hoped it would bring. As in the past, they would most likely return with a negotiator and the ransom, toward the end of summer. If the amount was enough, and then agreed upon, Brigit, Nora, and the negotiator would be returned as soon as possible.

Freyja sighed and pointed at Brigit when she caught Klause's eye. "So, you bring the little sister?" Klause teased Freyja, grabbing on to the horse's mane.

"Oh *Odin*! Please do not use these words. She is my sister, but not my charge," said Freyja a bit too earnestly. Brigit was lagging behind and scouring the crowd, taking in the busy scene. Freyja wondered if her sister realized that this was all because of her. All the furious preparations and risk of voyage to get her ransom, the girl with the silver chain. "The girl you speak of has indeed been sent with me for the day." Klause rolled his eyes in imitation of Freyja.

One man who had been loading the boat came forward to listen in and sat on a rock. Freyja turned to him. "I am here to wish *Frigga's* blessings on you and your voyage. 'Unharmed go forth, Unharmed return, Unharmed safe home.' Our farm sends bounty to share and comfort you." She laughed and pushed her bags into his arms.

"We are thankful for your blessings and your bounty. Perhaps we will see you at the Mead House after we are finished here?"

"Today we will go back to the farm. We continue our training these last days with Tahir before you depart," Freyja. replied. She turned the horse and motioned to Brigit to come with her. Brigit scanned the men around the ship and turned back with a disappointed look on her face.

"Yes, shield-maidens must always be learning and ready!" Klause laughed. Freyja stuck her tongue out at him knowing that their shared history may be part of the reason that Klause did not now take her seriously.

Chapter Ten

When the girls got back to the farm, they heard everyone inside involved in a loud discussion. The girls went inside to see Arndis going through the shelves.

Gunnar and Nora disappeared into her room and soon Nora was heard crying. Gunnar came out of the room with the belongings he kept there. "You were told that you did not have to go. There are enough men. They will be fine without you," Nora pleaded while blocking his path.

Gunnar looked down into her eyes filling with tears. "I have felt the pull of this, woman. I need to be part of this ransom voyage. Og and now Tahir need me to help them. I have navigated these waters before. I know the currents well and will help the trip greatly," replied Gunnar. Nora had to dry her eyes and nod agreement with him. "I do not mean to hurt your heart, but I need to help with the preparations. Just think of our reunion upon my return," smiled Gunnar and hugged Nora closely. "You will be well with the protection of your shield-maidens and it is only for the summer." Gunnar embraced Freyja, and then Brigit, saying goodbye and admonishing them to keep training.

Arndis put bread and cheese into his pack and nodded her goodbye. "We will come to send the ship when you are ready to leave. We listen for the horn," said Arndis.

"Tell them I will come to the village when it is full moon, to feast and leave with the ship," Tahir yelled to Gunnar as he left. "Now Arndis, we have some days still to make sweet so the goodbyes will not be so bitter," said Tahir. The Old One had cast the runes to choose Tahir to join this voyage as 'Og's right hand' and he was eager to help the village that had embraced him when Arndis did.

Each night when the moon rose, Tahir would take note of its roundness. The men had agreed to gather in the village with the full moon, but each man may mark its fullness differently. There would be a feast and then they would be off to the Far Isle. Arndis looked up at the moon and willed it to slow its waxing.

The following afternoons were filled with training. Every part of Freyja's body was challenged, with muscle building, resulting in nightly aches. Arndis had both girls sit near the fire to bake at night. She got them to sweat then rubbed their arms and backs.

"Oh, I did not know my arms could burn so," wailed Brigit. "They hurt each night, Tahir," she glowered at Tahir.

"They were very small when you first came. Now look at them. You grow before our eyes," Freyja laughed, then winced as she massaged her own arms.

"What about you Freyja? Do you not feel the pain and burning?" Brigit asked.

"No. I have decided to feel no pain. Like a wild *bezerker*!" Freyja said through clenched teeth. Brigit looked at her doubtfully. "Of course, I am in pain. Mother, do we have mead, that our pain may be lessened?" Freyja stuck out her bottom lip and made a pitiful face.

"All right. We have some I have saved and now seems like a good time for it. I tire of listening to the plight of you two shield-maidens in training," Arndis teased.

"What of the trainer? I too have worked very hard each day to help these girls," Tahir asked. He hugged her from behind and planted a kiss on Arndis' cheek while she smiled and shook her head. She filled cups for everyone to enjoy at the evening fire.

One morning Tahir declared that it was time to go. "The moon is round and if it is not full, it will soon be," he told all the women. They helped him pack his things and prepared three rabbits, cheese, and many roots to contribute to the feast. They loaded the horse and walked beside. Arndis and Tahir spoke quietly and Freyja and Brigit chatted with Nora. When they got to the village it seemed that most had agreed, the moon was full.

It was slow and soggy getting provisions to the ship with slush and mud on the path. Halig used his sledge and had brought a load more quickly. All day, more men arrived and the work was more quickly done. They would leave with the tide in the morning.

The men loaded the ship while the women prepared the feast. The feast for the ship's departure would also be their celebration for *Sumarmál* or Summer Time. It had been three moons since the last season's festival of Mid-Winter Night. They would now have six moons before the festivals of the seasons began again.

The children seemed to be always underfoot and watched as Og supervised butchering a steer for the sacrifice and feast. As the men returned from outfitting the ship, feasting began in earnest and drink was plentiful. The Old One cast the runes and portended a fruitful voyage. "All will be well and our village will prosper from this venture and newborn alliances," she declared.

"*Freyja, ask what you may do in my name.*" It was her goddess, so she asked the Old One. "What may I do for *Mardoll,* daughter of *Njord* of the sea, to help this voyage?"

The Old One looked her up and down, a great smile coming to her face. "Ahh, yes. You will learn much more. You will carve a rune stick for the voyage and in the morning place it on the ship with a blessing." Freyja was instructed to get a stick and cut it smooth for writing on. She then copied the runes as instructed by the Old One to create a blessing for the ship. "Now add your blood," directed the Old One handing Freyja her knife. Freyja cut her hand and used her finger to paint the lines of the runes red. As Freyja handed the finished stick to her, the Old One reached out to place her other hand on top of Freyja's head. She mumbled some words then smacked Freyja's head. She took this as a good omen as the Old One smiled and laughed uproariously.

After the feasting the girls walked back to the farm to care for the animals. Arndis and Nora wanted to stay and the girls promised to be back to see the ship off.

In the morning, the girls hurried with their chores and brought more food stuffs to donate to the voyage. Their walk was quick and they met others on their way to the beach. Arndis and Nora walked arm in arm, consoling each other. After all, it was a ransom negotiation trip, not a raid. Helga was looking proud and worried at the same time. She was wringing her hands and smiling too widely. She had delivered more than the promised bread and told everyone who would listen. Others had also come through with their donations. The ship seemed very well outfitted.

The Old One grabbed Freyja's arm to aid her walk to the water's edge. "I wish *Frigg's* blessing on this ship. Unharmed go forth, unharmed return, unharmed safe home," she said. She held out the rune stick in both hands and spoke to the sky. "AllFather protect our men. Their voyage is to the Far Isle to get ransom for this girl who is now more than a captive. This makes her worth greater and we will prosper." She handed the stick to Freyja and nodded.

"Lady Freyja, *Mardoll*, we ask *Njord's* guidance through the bright waters. Bring this ship home in victory." Freyja waded out to hand the stick to Og on board the ship. Og took it solemnly and the men raised their oars.

The ship rose with the foam of the coming tide and many ran to push it off. Laughter and tears mixed as they were hailed good voyage. Freyja, Arndis, and Nora watched, as the sail was raised, until the ship got smaller and finally disappeared. It seemed that Brigit had gone back to the village with the others.

The women gathered their things at the Mead House and loaded the horse. Arndis and Nora were tired and wanted to go so Freyja said she would come later with Brigit.

Many were gathering their things from the Mead House to return to their homes. Others were enjoying the food left from last night's feast. Freyja offered to help clean up from the festivities and found herself working with the long-haired slave woman, Fereshte. They gathered wooden plates and cups and gently roused the old brothers to send them home. "Hallr, Kofri! The ship is gone and it is time you were home." Freyja said as they helped the old brothers up. They had eaten, drunk, and now rested well.

"Did all go well with their leaving?" asked Kofri.

"Yes," said Freyja. "The way was clear of ice and they caught the tide and wind. We saw their sail full as they met the horizon."

"It is well," said Hallr. "Now to home!"

"We will go with you," offered Brigit with Sven.

"Yes," said the brothers together as they each took one of Brigit's arms. Sven followed as an afterthought.

Freyja busied herself with more cleaning up and noticed Brigit and Sven had returned. They were alone, seated by the fire. They spoke in low tones and smiled often at each other. Freyja shook her head. She had thought it strange that The Old One had insisted upon Sven staying in the village instead of joining in the ransom voyage.

Fereshte asked Freyja to help take some things up to the loft. They each carried several bags up the ladder and stored the items away. Freyja stood at the edge of the loft, looking down at Brigit and Sven. They held hands and laughed. She heard Fereshte come up behind her and then felt a hand lift the hair from the side of her neck. Soft lips caressed her neck. "Leave them," Fereshte whispered.

This was more than an instruction to ignore the love below her. It was wise counsel to loose her heart from old entanglements. But the kisses upon her neck were surprising and the nearness of this beautiful woman offering comfort was something new.

An arm encircled Freyja's waist and she was pulled close. The warmth of the soft kisses on her neck was exquisite. A dizzying array of thoughts flooded her mind.

Red Eric had been a surprising addition to her love life this past summer. When his ship had come to trade, bringing Tahir back to the village, she had believed that love would never be hers again. Now more love was being offered to her and by a woman?

Gently, she was turned around and pulled away from the edge. Fereshte bent down to grab Freyja's apron dress to pull it over her head. When Freyja's arms were above her, Fereshte put her warm mouth on Freyja's and kissed her deeply. Freyja wrenched her arms free of her dress to toss it down and wrap her newly freed arms around the woman, without shame. They stayed like that for a long time. Kissing and holding each other tightly. The warmth building between them.

Fereshte broke off the kisses to take Freyja by the hand and lead her to the bench against the wall that was her bed. She pulled up Freyja's under gown and pushed her so her bare skin sat on soft furs. Then Freyja felt her under dress being pulled over her head. Fereshte removed her own dress and knelt in front of Freyja to put her face in Freyja's breasts. Her mouth sought the textures and Freyja gasped. The woman obviously had knowledge of the female body and Freyja wondered aloud, "You have done this before?"

"Shhhh," Fereshte put her finger on Freyja's lips. Fereshte climbed up to straddle Freyja's hips and helped her lie back upon the bed. Fereshte then rolled over next to Freyja in the bed and touched her gently. She was instructing her as to the wonders of flesh, bringing intense pleasure. She reached out to grab Freyja's hand and brought it to herself. Freyja used her understanding of her own body to pleasure Fereshte. They both felt fulfilled and held each other tenderly. The dark-haired beauty fell asleep quickly, but Freyja lay awake. What was this to be, she wondered? Did this mean something between the two women or had the goddess of sexuality given her this unique experience to teach her something?

CHAPTER ELEVEN

F reyja woke to hear voices below the loft and peeked
over to see Fereshte sweeping then serving some stew
to Sven and Brigit. She looked at the beautiful dark-haired
woman and wondered about her past life. She knew that
she, Freyja, must be linked to a man in the future. If she
married or if she became a concubine of a married man,
she might have loving relationships with other women as
long as she fulfilled the duty of reproducing for a man's
lineage. Sex with any, of age, was a pleasure, to be sure,
but bearing children was truly the life blood of their culture.
She wondered if Fereshte's culture was anything like hers.
She also wondered, as she ran her hand through her hair,
how she had learned her skills in lovemaking.

Fereshte looked up to see Freyja and waived happily,
motioning for her to come down. She kissed Freyja on
the cheek at the bottom of the ladder and handed her a
bowl of stew. They sat together with Sven and Brigit eating
peacefully.

Sven pushed his empty bowl back and stood to leave.
He whispered something in Brigit's ear and nodded his
farewell to the others. When he reached the doorway,

Brigit ran after him. A few moments later she returned to sit down, breathless and flushed. Freyja raised her eyebrows at the girl and she blushed. She opened her mouth to speak, then pinched her lips together, shook her head and was silent.

"We must to the farm, Brigit. They will think we have been lost," Freyja spoke with a kind voice. Brigit nodded and gathered her things. She went outside while Freyja helped Fereshte take the bowls from the table. The women exchanged a genuinely warm hug and smiled goodbye looking into each other's eyes.

Both Brigit and Freyja were silent on the walk home. They picked some late berries and mushrooms, seemingly lost in their thoughts. Once in a while Brigit would hum and hug herself slightly. Freyja could imagine her thoughts and only smiled.

Once home they were greeted with a list of things to do. Cow milk to be made into butter. Goat milk to be made into cheese. The whey from both to be used to pickle roots. Freyja thought about arguing and then realized that she had missed a day's work on the farm in exchange for love in the loft. She agreed with a nod and began working near the fire. Brigit did not argue either and Freyja wondered what her night had been like, just for a moment. She bit her lip and decided that she really did not want to know.

The girls did all that Arndis and Nora could think for them to do and at *nattmal* all the women seemed content. "I know that market days will be small for a time, but having something to trade will still do well for us," Ardnis said with a pleased nod. She and Nora had spent the day after the ship left resting so she wanted to catch up on work.

"It is good, Mother. I am happy to make food for us," replied Freyja around a mouthful of bread and soft goat cheese.

"Yes," said Brigit. "The happy goats make very good cheese," she smiled. They relaxed and Nora started singing a song from her homeland. She and Brigit danced a bit while Arndis and Freyja looked on. They praised the song and dance and Arndis wished everyone good night. Nora soon went to her bed and Freyja waited for moon rise.

It was still enough of a full moon for her purposes and she took Brigit to the meadow and approached her altar. She found the stone that was hers still standing beside the black stone that represented Brigit. She handed Brigit her stone and took her own in her hands. Holding it tightly to her chest she called on the goddess *Freyja* to hear her. "Lady, I ask that you watch over our ship and men as they go to negotiate ransom for Brigit. Please bring them back safely across the waters, *Mardoll*. I thank you for accepting me and for the learning coming from the Old One. I will honor you as a shield-maiden."

When Freyja looked at Brigit, she saw that she too held her stone and whispered her own invocations. They stood quietly for some time, bathed in moonlight. There was a gentle breeze and it was pleasant to be in the meadow. Freyja noted that it was also pleasant to spend time with Brigit, her sister. "I wonder at your leaving now. At first, I wanted you to be gone and out of my life. Now I learn from you and laugh with you," Freyja looked at her feet as she admitted this.

"Yes," nodded Brigit with a hesitant smile. "I too feel troubled by the thought of leaving more than staying."

Freyja took her stone and placed it on the altar. She motioned Brigit to do the same. Her toe bumped into a stone and she reached down to find the long-forgotten Sven stone. She laughed and held it out to Brigit. "This stone is Sven. I used to keep it next to my stone. Now you may put it next to yours." Brigit gasped audibly, but took the stone in her hands. She solemnly placed the stone on the other side of hers, far away from the Freyja stone.

"You know?" Brigit asked her sister.

"Yes." Freyja said with a smirk. She raised one eyebrow and took Brigit by the arm to walk back to the farm.

Now they began a new routine. Up with the sun to tend to cows, goats, chickens, then *dagmal* together at the fire. Then there was tending of the garden, wildcrafting for edible plants and herbs, and checking the rabbit snares. Training continued at the forest's edge using the stickmen and some sparring between each other. Nora had devised some clever wrist protection from rabbit pelts. At sunset they would gather for *nattmal* and share time around the fire, telling stories or jokes and singing. They were teaching each other songs though they often laughed at each other's accents.

A few weeks after the ship left, the old brothers appeared on Sven's horse with Sven and Fereshte walking beside. They had brought Freyja's shield, now mended, and wanted to see how training was going. Hallig had sent Fereshte to purchase some cheese from Arndis.

"Thank you, brothers of the forge. This is a great gift," Freyja gasped as she looked over the shield. She took them to see the stickmen. She felt a little awkward showing her skills in front of Sven, but Fereshte stepped forward to pick up a wooden practice sword and sparred with her. Sven did the same with Brigit and soon they had all worked up a sweat.

Arndis and Nora arrived from washing clothes at the creek and insisted that the training stop so that they might join in on the visiting. They bustled about and soon cheese was presented to the brothers along with some mead they had saved. Nora hurried to make some bread by the fire.

"To the brothers and their skill of the forge," Arndis toasted.

"Yes," said all, together. Brigit excused herself at sunset to tend to the animals and Sven followed. Freyja decided to show Fereshte the farm while the brothers rested by the fire telling old stories to a new audience.

Fereshte reached for Freyja's arm as they walked and soon slid her hand down to interlace their fingers. Such a sweet gesture caught Freyja off guard. When they got to the stickmen Freyja adjusted the front of one and Fereshte went to the back to help reshape it. They peeked around the same side at the same moment and Freyja was met with a warm kiss on the mouth. She fell into warm, waiting arms and they sat upon the earth kissing and holding each other for a long time. Coming up for breath, Freyja suggested getting a sleeping skin for the evening and they walked back to the house.

Nora was giving her bed to the brothers and she would sleep in with Arndis. "The young ones will work things out for themselves," she said handing a skin each to Freyja and Fereshte.

"Thank you, Nora. We will spend the night with *Mani* and wake with his sister, *Sol.*" Freyja ushered Fereshte down the steps toward the meadow. When they got there, Brigit was standing before the altar with Sven. She held his hand and touched their stones with the other. Freyja tried to make no noise as they passed, but they were heard by the couple. Brigit turned to see the two women and Freyja motioned silently that they were continuing down the path to the creek. Brigit smiled her thanks.

Mani, the moon deity, led them to the perfect spot. They placed their furs on a small rise up from the creek where they could hear the rushing water. They snuggled close between the sleeping skins. As they warmed, they began to remove their outer clothing. It was a surprise to feel bare skin against bare skin and Freyja's chest tingled. She pressed her breasts against Fereshte's. Their legs soon wrapped around each other. Their lips sought each other's and hands explored. Finally, exhausted from their passion they began to talk, as they could lying side by side.

With Freyja's arms around Fereshte, she looked at the upturned dark eyes and asked, "How long have you been the slave of Halig?"

"I have been with Halig for seven cycles of winter and summer," replied Fereshte. Her voice grew somber and she lowered her eyes. She began to kiss Freyja's neck.

Freyja pulled back. "I have been told of your sword and your freedom to come, by the old brothers," Freyja pried as she searched the other woman's face. "You will have these both one day." Freyja's voice was hopeful.

Fereshte's eyes began to shine with fervor. She sat up to look down on Freyja. "I will be free in one more season. I will take back my sword and return to my home," she said. "I will have honor again." She sighed and lay down with her back to Freyja.

Freyja curled around her, "Tell me of your dream of freedom," she whispered into Fereshte's ear.

She rolled to face Freyja. "I will find those who travel toward my home and go where the fruit is sweet and the air is warm. I will be among those who will not stare at me. I will seek out a place where women can still wield a sword and be of honorable service." She yawned loudly and snuggled into Freyja with a small smile on her face.

Freyja woke with the sun on her face and rain? She squinted her eyes to look up and find Fereshte shaking her wet hair over her. She had bathed in the creek. "Wake Freyja. *Sol* warms us. You should wash," Fereshte laughed. She pulled on Freyja's arm and laughed while running to the creek. Freyja followed with gaining enthusiasm as she watched the playful nymph. They both waded in and splashed each other while washing quickly in the cold water. Freyja ran back to the skins and buried her cold, wet body within them. Fereshte followed and they shivered a bit together. They laughed as they cuddled to warm each other, their skin slipping and sliding. They lay back snuggling then Fereshte dove under the fur skins. Freyja's eyes widened as she felt new sensations with Fereshte between her legs. Reaching down her hands found Fereshte's head and her fingers curled tightly in her hair. She gripped the thick dark hair as she shuddered.

Fereshte climbed up to kneel across Freyja, encouraging her in kind. Freyja hesitated then found a new experience. Fereshte moved until she drew in quick breaths and panting, climbed between the furs. They lay together for a few moments, then energized, Freyja pulled Fereshte up and they ran to the creek once again. This time, after they washed each other, they dressed and began the walk to the farm.

Freyja told of her childhood and Fereshte followed her pointed finger to note the locations spoken of. When Freyja stopped to touch a tree Fereshte picked up her hand to place a kiss upon her palm.

At the meadow they noticed a large impression left in the grass. Freyja smiled and wondered at the one they must have left behind near the creek.

In front of the house, they saw Sven and Brigit embrace. "Come Freyja, we are to our chores," said Brigit when she saw them approach. She pushed Sven toward the door. Freyja motioned for Fereshte to join Sven and the girls went together to the barn. They cared for the cows, horse, and goats then released them to the farm yard. The cows and horse would graze on what they could find and the goats would seek any plants within reach. They hunted for eggs and each found a handful to carry inside.

Inside they found the old brothers, Hallr and Kofri, enjoying more cheese and freshly baked bread. Nora laughed as she broke another round of bread for them to share and brought out the butter.

"You are fed well at our farm. We are glad of your company and 'a gift always looks for a gift'. We are thankful for your gifts of weapons to Brigit and repairs to Freyja's," said Arndis affably.

Freyja and Brigit put the eggs in a pot and added water for them to boil. They sat next to Fereshte and Sven respectively and ate with them. There was joking and laughter. "Brothers, I am sorry to say, but I must be home to my farm," said Sven. The brothers brushed off crumbs and each reached for an arm to help them up, sighing.

Kofri bowed slightly, "Thank you to the beautiful women of this farm. Your hospitality has been a gift, indeed."

Hallr nodded in agreement, "We hope to see you when next you come to market. Bring cheese and we will trade."

Arndis quickly wrapped some cheese in a cloth to send with them. "This will keep you until next we see you," said Arndis kissing them each on one cheek.

Brigit and Freyja each helped a brother out of the house. They stretched their legs at the well and mounted the horse. Sven and Fereshte started walking and they all looked back to wave goodbye. Brigit looked as if she wished to follow.

The women of the farm, settled back into their routine with one exception. Every week or so Freyja and/or Brigit would volunteer to go to market and trade for them. Arndis and Nora did not mind as the village was fairly quiet, there would be little news or gossip. Besides both of their men were on the voyage so they were happy to stay on the farm. Nora had discovered Grandmother's loom. In recent trades she had acquired thread and instructed the girls to get more in order for her to weave.

On trips to the village, the girls would trade and end up at the Mead House where the old brothers would buy them a cup of mead or ale. Then, most often, they would stay the night with their respective lovers. Walking home, Freyja would sing a song that Fereshte had taught her and Brigit would daydream. They never spoke of it, but each knew that they were falling in love.

Chapter Twelve

A nother moon cycle passed and all the women seemed happy with their arrangement. The warm weather lifted all their spirits. When they had enough to trade, the girls were sent to do it. The older women suspected that love was what kept them over night on these trips. They let it be and did not speak of it.

Often one of the women would climb the rocky prominence to look at the beach and the landing spot. They knew it was early for the ship's return, but Freyja especially enjoyed the reenactment of her childhood search for her grandfather. She would note the height of the tide and what had washed up recently on their shore.

One morning she did this after checking her rabbit snares. She left the four freshly caught rabbits at the bottom of the rocky prominence and climbed up, eager to see the beautiful vista. Once up she gasped and her hands shook as she fumbled for her flint.

A ship had landed and a group of men started up the path toward the village. It was not their ship and these men were armed. She looked closer at the beach below and saw a second bunch of men walking toward the path to her own farm. It was clearly a raiding party, but she could not imagine what they hoped to find. She hurriedly lit the signal fire and scrambled down the rocky outcropping, forgetting her rabbits.

She ran to the farm yelling on her approach, "A raiding party is coming. Some to the village and some to the farm," her voice started to shake then she remembered her pledge to protect her people. Now was the time to honor it and she and Brigit had been training for just this sort of thing. "Brigit and I will start to the village. Mother, take Nora, ride to the twin's farm, and light their signal fire, then you must hide them and yourselves," she barked these instructions.

Brigit dropped the eggs she had gathered and grabbed her weapons. Freyja put on her new belt with dagger and sword sheaths and added the dagger and sword. Then, grabbing her axe and shield, she ran to catch up with Brigit who, with her own weapons, had already started walking. In moments Nora and Arndis passed them, galloping on the horse. They soon took the path to the other farm and all called out blessings of safety and luck. Freyja picked up their pace being careful to watch for others.

To their side, in the forest, they saw one of Helga's slaves and ran to her. "Go to Helga to say raiders are coming to the village," Freyja spoke quickly.

"I go," replied the girl who started toward the village, down the path.

"No," hissed Brigit. "Go through the forest so you will not be seen. Especially take care when crossing the road. Tell all you meet to prepare." The girl nodded and ran off through the woods.

Freyja did not often travel through the forest, but it was a familiar enough trek that they soon approached the village. They could hear fighting and commotion as soon as their faces brushed past the last branches of evergreens surrounding the town. They neared the doorway to the Mead House and could see Halig at the door fighting off an intruder. Brigit drew her sword and attacked from behind. The intruder quickly wheeled around to engage her, stepping out in the open. Freyja slipped behind him to enter and take stock of what was going on. Someone was in the back, loading supplies on to the owner Halig's cart. Halig slumped to sit against the wall with his hand to his side. In another corner it looked like someone had Fereshte pinned down on the ground. She was pounding him with her fists on his back and kicking wildly as he tried to push her legs apart. Freyja ran to them, grabbed the man by the hair and put her dagger to his neck. When she lifted his head a line of red beaded up on the bare skin below his beard. He turned his head and she could see his face. It was Red Eric. Freyja let out a low wild howl and vehemently slit his throat. He collapsed on Fereshte and Freyja pulled him off. She bent down to check on her friend just as two more raiders entered the building.

Freyja sheathed her dagger and raised her sword, standing protectively in front of Fereshte. Halig tried to stand with his sword to fight. He pushed with his legs, trying to rise up the wall, but his wound was too great and his strength too little. He slid down the wall and gazed at Fereshte. With a meaningful look he jerked his head toward her sword where it was always displayed, on the back wall. The sword promised to be returned to her in one year's time along with her freedom.

Fereshte gave out a curdling scream and bounded up on to a nearby table. She leapt on the ladder to the loft with one foot, then spun in midair, grabbing her curved sword off the wall. She landed on top of a table in a crouch, sword in hand, ready for battle. She leapt into the fray and she and Freyja took on the two intruders. Freyja could keep them occupied, but it was Fereshte who disarmed them. She inflicted several small wounds on each so they could not use their weapons. The men gave up, sinking to the floor. The women took their weapons and sat the men against a wall. They tipped a table, on its side, across their legs to keep them still. Halig watched over the captured men as the women went out front.

Sven had appeared and joined Brigit. They were fighting with three or four men. Fereshte did not hesitate and engaged them. Freyja picked one to focus on and soon had his sword. She marched him into the Mead House at the point of his own sword.

Halig spoke hoarsely, "Go to the back to bar the other door."

Freyja did and returned. "Your cart is now gone, with your supplies," she reported. He shook his head sadly and winced in pain. Fereshte, Brigit, and Sven entered, each with a captive. The pile of weapons was growing as they disarmed the men.

"We know these men, Freyja," said Brigit between heaving breaths.

"Yes," said Freyja. "There lies Red Eric, who is now as red as his name. I had to kill him." Her stomach clenched and she felt she might vomit.

Brigit's eyes widened and she gasped. "These are the men from the ship who brought Tahir!" Brigit shook her head in disbelief.

"The thieves who once stole the wine I bought from them have now taken my cart with all else of my goods," Halig panted. Fereshte went to him to comfort him and see about his wound. They heard voices approaching from outside and Sven stood inside out of sight, to the side of the door.

Freyja stepped out of the doorway seeing Lek, and several more from the ship, leading a line of captives. The twins, their mother and their female slave from the neighboring farm were bound by their hands. Nora, and Arndis were with them. All their waists were tied, as slaves often are, to a long rope being led by a young man. "We have Red Eric and others inside as our captives," yelled Freyja.

"Freyja, it is good to see you," sneered Lek. Fereshte stepped out on recognizing his voice. "And you, my sweet, armed with your play sword."

Freyja kept talking to Lek as she watched a group of villagers sneak up behind the men from the forest. Helga was at the front of the group, with a sword in her hand, looking angrily at Lek. "You will not take our people to your ship. Our ancestral spirits, the *Nonir*, have woven them into our lives," Freyja stated.

"Ha, I will take as I please," Lek spat on the ground. Helga ran up behind him and swung her sword. It was too heavy for her and she only slapped him with it. Angrily Lek turned to grab her by her hair to hold her in front of him, his sword at her throat. "One angry old woman will not fetch much as a slave, but I will take her with the others to Hedeby and we will see," laughed Lek.

The crowd behind him surged forward to attack and Freyja, Fereshte, Sven, and Brigit joined them. The two groups surrounded the men from the ship and kept them busy. Brigit came up behind the young man holding the captives' rope and held her sword to his neck. He dropped the rope and Arndis used his knife to cut her bindings and then set all free.

The freed captives picked up rocks and pelted the men mercilessly with them. Helga stomped on Lek's feet and butted him with her ample buttocks until he let her go. With the front of Lek exposed Fereshte ran in to engage him.

She took out her anger at him for betraying her and all the village. She landed many blows on his arms from the sharp tip of her curved scimitar. It took a toll and he slowed in his responses. They fought a focused battle in front of the Mead House.

Lek's attention was drawn by another rock thrown at him and he turned. Getting behind him Fereshte sliced his sword shoulder and he dropped his sword. He knelt on one knee to retrieve it. As she came around to his front, sword raised, he picked his sword up with his other hand and ran it up and into her chest. At the same time, she brought her sword down to cleave his neck at the shoulder. He stood with a last bit of energy, wrapping his arm around her, and they clung together as his life blood drained out. Their knees buckled and both slumped to the ground. Fereshte removed his hand from his sword and pushed him away. She went down on one knee then lay back upon the ground reddening with her blood. Sword in hand.

During the battle Brigit and Sven had worked as a team to each wear down an opponent and then traded at the last moment to surprise their prey. Sven had killed two of the other men with Brigit's help in this way. Freyja had wounded several.

As the fighting ended, the battle-weary crowd closed in to drag the wounded to the wall of the Mead House. The dead were left with Fereshte laying among them. Freyja noticed the dark head of hair among the others and ran to her side. She quickly kneeled to take her hand.

"Your wound is not bad and you will heal quickly," she told Fereshte the lie. She straightened out her loves twisted legs and held her head on her lap. Fereshte laughed weakly and shook her head, knowing that her wound was mortal. Freyja spoke earnestly, "We have stopped these slave traders because of you. Because of you, the twins will grow up on their farm and I will have my mother." The tears came to her eyes and rolled down her face. Freyja kissed her love's face and rocked her in her arms. "You have brought love to my life and I cannot let you go." She smiled.

Fereshte smiled up at her. "You must ask my master how to send me on. My death must be done rightly. My body will be left, then three days later, buried."

Freyja tried to keep a confused look off her face and nodded. "We will do as you ask."

Fereshte reached up with both hands to cup Freyja's face and looked deeply into her eyes with love. "Thank you," she sighed and closed her eyes. Freyja continued to rock her as she held her tightly, crying softly, alone.

All the village had withdrawn respectfully into the Mead House and pulled the wounded inside. Most of the men from the ship had been injured, but many wounds were very small. Brigit and Nora were tending to them using a knowledge of healing that they had not shown before. Arndis had collected all the weapons in one pile. The old brothers had been among the crowd and now looked over the haul of weapons. They waved their hands about and nodded as they discussed these.

Helga had taken charge of the twins and several other girls to pull pouches and items off the bodies and wounded. They searched them diligently for items of value. One of the twins yelled excitedly, *"Brisingamen, Brisingamen,* Helga!" Waving the amber necklace, she had found on Red Eric, she ran to Helga who joyfully snatched it from her hands.

Helga waved the necklace, laughing, "The necklace comes back to me and the thief has come to justice, thank

Odin." She put it on and continued to laugh, twirling in front of all.

Klause took a few boys with him to the raiders' ship with the idea of sinking it. With so many men now being their captives, they worried that an escape could be carried out too easily. They carried axes with them to hack a few holes in the hull.

First, they took down the sail and loaded the cargo on the cart to bring back to the village. While searching through the ship they found a man hiding. "Thank the gods you have saved me," a voice called out from among some bags.

"Karle! It is you. We thought you might have been taken for a slave by Eric and it seems so," Klause spoke. Relieved, he offered Karle his arm to pull him out of the ship.

Karle dusted himself off and greeted the men from his village. "I have returned, but with few tales as I was not with the ship long. Still, I might make a poem of my journey," Karle smiled brightly.

When the cart got to the back door of the Mead House it was opened happily. All goods were returned to their owners, but there were many more items on the ship. These were passed out evenly among the people. The brother Hallr was thrilled to get a skin of wine, as was Nora. There were also dried fruits, nuts, and some wonderful sharp daggers made of a miracle ore. The brother Kofri got one of the daggers, as well as Sven and Brigit. One was set aside for Freyja and given to Arndis to hold, as Freyja was still outside with Fereshte in her arms.

Karle's mother screamed when she saw him enter. She thrust her baby into her husband's arms and ran to her son. "My son, you are safe. Hail the gods. We knew you must have been taken as a slave by Red Eric. I had grieved for you already."

The Old One looked relieved, but not entirely convinced of Karle's innocence. "I believed that you had desecrated the god post of our Lady. I hoped that I was wrong," she ventured.

Just then, Freyja looked through the doorway to see Karle. He reached to the bag at his belt and pulled out the necklace to hand to the Old One. Karle explained, "Just as you say. Eric took me and forced me to tell of any treasure. Here is the necklace." He smiled to all as he held it out.

When he reached for his bag, he threw back his cloak which revealed the stolen *seax* hanging from his belt as well. The Old One grabbed the necklace and stepped back in horror.

Freyja stood and walked woodenly toward the door. She screamed, "I curse you Karle. I doom you to *Niflheim* for theft from the goddess *Freyja*. You have desecrated her god post and stolen gifts given in sacred *blot*. Gifts I was entrusted with by the shield-maiden wight. I curse you for stealing from the *landvaettir* on our journey to Rocky Peak as well. You have stolen from your gods and your people. You are no longer welcome in your own home or village." Freyja began chanting under her breath. She slowly pointed both arms at him and an energy seemed to build from her fingertips toward Karle.

Karle laughed as he pulled the *seax* from his belt. "Only the precious Freyja and Sven find favor with the gods, so I take what I want. This gift from the shield-maiden will find its home in your heart, girl." He took a step toward Freyja who clapped her hands together. His next step seemed as if his feet were in quick clay and he slipped. Next, both of Freyja's palms came up as to block him. Karle began to run as he tried to keep himself upright still slipping. Just as he neared Freyja in the doorway her wrists and elbows bent forcefully down. Karle's body twisted in a grotesque manner and he fell to the ground on his belly.

Blood began to seep from his open mouth as he lay prostrate in front of Freyja. His mother ran to him screaming and flailing her hands above his back. Finally, she grabbed his shoulder to turn him over. He had fallen upon the *seax* and impaled himself through the gut.

Freyja collapsed in a daze. After a moment of staring at nothing she crawled back to Fereshte's body to sit with her back to the Mead House, rocking slowly.

The Old One's face was ashen. She covered her head with her shawl and held it tightly under her chin with one hand. The other held the necklace of amber and gold that Freyja had been given by the ghost of a shield-maiden. She left the Mead House and her closest relatives followed in silence. She did not look at Karle and walked past Freyja without a word.

Karle's mother screamed, "Someone pull this weapon from my son. We must avenge him, ask for *wergeld,* appeal to the gods." Karle's father held their baby and took the other children quickly out the door.

All the people turned their backs as one on her. They looked to be in shock though they had seen death many times before. Karle's mother rocked her bloodied child in her arms, alone.

Halig motioned his male servants to carry Karle's body outside with the others. One took the woman's elbow to help her stand as they lifted him. Karle's mother followed outside dejectedly. She looked around as though searching. After some moments she began to walk toward her farm, dragging her feet.

Inside, the wounded had been moved against one wall and the people sat in silence for a long time. Brigit began to pass out cups and people began to talk softly. They made a somber meal in the Mead House of the abundant food from the ship, then departed for their homes. They had decided that the captives would be given out to some as slaves until their own men came home. Helga had one in tow on a rope. Her original slaves were smiling, almost dancing, as they would now have help on the farm. The twins' mother took the youngest man to their farm hoping he would help with the late harvest while her husband was gone. Arndis declined to have a slave at their farm. "I want no man to care for unless he is of my choosing." She, Nora, and Brigit took their spoils and looked for the horse. He was nearby grazing and did not seem at all bothered by the day's events.

The women noted Freyja had returned to sit beside the body of Fereshte. She was singing a song from Fereshte's home with her eyes closed as she stroked her hair. Arndis came to kneel next to her. "You must prepare her for *Vallhalla*," she said softly, putting her hand on Freyja's shoulder.

"I must speak to her master as she asked. It is different with her people." Freyja opened her eyes and nodded sadly, gently taking her hands from Fereshte. Arndis extended her hand to pull her daughter up off the ground as she also stood.

Arndis hugged her daughter, "We will come when we are called by the horn." The women left Freyja with her task. When they looked back, she was still standing beside the body, silent tears still falling.

CHAPTER THIRTEEN

Halig surveyed the Mead House from his seat. It would take some time to clean the mess and repair the damage and he had lost his most loved and trusted servant. Fereshte had been thought of as more of a friend. When he had captured her in battle everyone advised him to kill her or sell her as a slave. He had admired her bravery in battle and disliked the idea of what would await her in the slave markets and beyond. He had taken her for his own slave and they had made their unusual and honorable agreement seven years ago.

He had taken her weapon and had offered her the chance to earn it back. She would work for him for eight years or until his death, which ever came first. At that time, he would reward her service by giving her the title of a free woman and returning her scimitar. She had agreed with one addition; she did not wish to bed her master as most slaves were expected to do. He was taken aback by the request, but agreed as he respected her as a warrior. So, they had begun their working arrangement and when he returned to the village with her, she worked honorably beside him always to the best of her ability. Halig rose unsteadily to his feet and made his way to the door, holding on to the wall. "Farewell, my friend," he said under his breath as he leaned against the doorway, looking at her body on the ground. Freyja had respectfully placed her sword in her hands and her hands upon her chest.

Freyja came to him, her faced streaked with tears. "We are to honor the death practices of her people, Halig. I have promised," she sighed. Klause stood and motioned another to join him. They went to the body and brought her inside to a table. Freyja looked to Halig for instruction.

"You will wash her body and wrap it loosely in white cloth. In the morning, we will take her to the rocks between the forest and the shore and let her lie there for the scavengers for three days." Freyja sucked in her breath audibly then her mouth twisted and she swallowed hard. She nodded to let him know she understood. Halig continued, "After three days you will collect her bones and bury them." He sat down heavily on a bench, his strength giving out.

Klause, Sven, and the last remaining villagers went home for the night. Halig gave them instructions as they left. "You will tell all who wish to honor Fereshte to come in the morning. We make a procession for her trip to her kind of *Valhalla*."

Sven stopped to speak softly to Freyja, "I will go to your farm to tell them of this." Freyja gripped his forearm but did not say anything as she looked into his eyes with great sadness. He gently took her hand from his arm and left.

Freyja tenderly washed Fereshte and wrapped her with cloth that had come from the ship. It was a fine linen to make a fine shroud. When she had done this Halig told her to place some lights around the body to ward off evil spirits. They used the oil lamps as there were no candles to be had. Once finished, Freyja sat next to Halig on the bench. He groaned with the movement.

"Halig, your wound is great!" Freyja exclaimed pulling his hand away. She opened his shirt to find a large gash below his ribs on one side. She tore his shirt away and washed his wound. In the back of the Mead House, she found herbs to make a pack for the wound, then wrapped his chest with more of the fine cloth. She found sheepskins to make a place for him against the wall and helped him to it. For several hours she dozed fitfully between watching Halig for fever and Fereshte for spirits. When the moon rose, its light shone through the open door and drew her. She stood to walk out into the cool breeze and silver light.

Evidence of the day's carnage showed in pools of blood and churned earth. Bodies lay strewn about and Karle's lay among them. Freyja's jaw clenched and she looked away quickly.

She turned her gaze and thoughts to the night stars. The fresh air soothed her and she opened her arms to bare her soul to the sky. "AllFather, gods all; I cry tonight and am in need of comfort. We have won the day, but we have lost so much. I have killed and I have seen others killed. Perhaps I did not do all that I could. I call on you to protect my people."

"My child, we hear you. We have always been by your side. That is why you prevailed today and why you continue on

Midgard. As my namesake and shield-maiden you have my protection."

Freyja sank to her knees and hugged herself. She felt the hug was from her goddess and was reassured as she cried fully and without shame. After all, she knew that tears are *Freyja's* gold. After a time, she went back inside and slept as if she had taken a potion, for the rest of the night.

By the morning Karle's body had disappeared. The tainted *seax* lay untouched on the ground in a pool of blood. Halig instructed his slaves to dig a mass grave for the others to be buried without ceremony.

The old warrior appeared to be somewhat better. He moved around slowly, holding his side. "Freyja, gather the lamps so that we may lift and load the body on the cart."

"You mean Fereshte. She has a name, even in death," Freyja glowered at Halig.

"Yes. Yes, Freyja. We take Fereshte to her place for these days." Freyja sighed shakily and put the lamps in the back of the room.

A boy entered carrying a horn. "Do I call the people to come now?" he asked.

"Yes," said Halig. "We will eat while we wait." The boy looked very happy and went outside to blow his horn. He came right back in, eager to be fed and see what Halig had to offer.

Halig had the boy bring out some food they had retrieved from the ship. There was still dried fruit and dried meats, wine, and mead. Halig and the boy set upon the food. Freyja had no appetite. She took a long drink of mead and stepped outside to wait. She kicked the dirt and walked in circles. It was a fine day, but she could see no beauty in it. She hated the idea of what they would do with Fereshte's body and wrung her hands thinking about it. She wondered how the people would take it as well.

After some time, the first of the people arrived. Helga with her household; the twin girls and their mother with their new slave; then Brigit, Arndis, and Nora. Others straggled in and spoke low in small groups. They knew this was not to be a Viking pyre and were apprehensive. The Old One arrived and walked a wide circle around the seax on the ground. She pointed to it and nodded to her grandson who picked it up by a cloth, wrapping it quickly.

Halig slowly brought his cart around and asked some boys to carry Fereshte's body to it. Freyja watched conflicted, wanting to manage things, but holding back. She took a step forward to help, then stopped. Thankfully, Halig began to speak.

"I have known Fereshte these seven years. She was a warrior from a faraway place with different traditions. We will follow them as we can." He shook his head slowly, eyes on the ground. "Grandmother," he spoke to the Old One. "Will you call our gods to join us and aid her as they will?"

The Old One stood and raised her staff to the sky. "*Odin*. Guide this warrior to *Valhalla* even though she has another name for it. We honor her sacrifice for our people and ask that she be accepted among the brave where she may live forever!" The Old One's voice rose to a fever pitch at the end encouraging all to join her cheer. "Hail Fereshte. Hail Fereshte. Hail Fereshte, may she live forever!"

Halig stepped forward. "Now we walk together to the shore. We must keep a quiet procession as is her tradition." People exchanged looks of confusion, eyebrows knitted, but began to follow the cart quietly. When they reached the shore, they could see the bandit ship sunken by the boys. Some were clapped on the back to show approval, but quietly. The cart stopped as it reached the soft sand and several boys stepped forward to carry Fereshte's body. Freyja came to the cart and reached out to carry a shoulder. Together, she and the boys lifted the shrouded corpse and carried Fereshte up into the rocks and laid her down gently amid the grasses. Freyja had brought along the scimitar and could not help herself. She laid it down beside Fereshte in hopes it would be near her for *Valhalla*, even if it was not appropriate. The people waited quietly.

Finally, Halig spoke. "In the tradition of Fereshte's people, her body will stay here three days as does her spirit. She will share her flesh with the scavengers," (there was a huge gasp from the crowd) "then her bones will be collected to be buried." People glanced from face to face nervously, with eyes wide. "Freyja and I will collect the bones and bury them," Halig explained. He put the crowd at ease and they stopped shifting their feet. "Now, we will go back to the village." The boys turned the cart around and pulled it back to the Mead House.

At the Mead House, once more the people seemed confused. Would there be a feast now or in seven days as for a Chieftain? The Old One came to speak with Halig and Freyja. "What shall we do?" she asked in a quiet voice.

"The people have come to honor Fereshte. We will feast as we can. Do you agree?" asked Freyja looking at them both.

"Yes," answered Halig. "We will share all from the ship and I will honor her as well with my stores." Halig turned to the people, "Tonight we honor Fereshte. Come, for we are her family." He motioned the people inside the Mead House. He and Freyja began to fill cups and pass them out. The action of serving helped to subdue Freyja's sorrow and connect her to her people once more. Everyone touched her shoulder or gripped her hand. Glasses were raised to toast Fereshte, her bravery in defending the village and her loving service to the people these many years.

As Freyja filled yet another mourner's cup with the red wine from the captured ship, she could not help but equate it with the life blood that had poured from the wounds of her sapphic lover. Her hands began to tremble and much wine splattered to the floor. She stood in silent stillness and let the visions of Fereshte come.

Fereshte had spoken of her years with Halig and the fact that she had only one year left of service. She had spoken warmly of returning to her homeland. Travel and the chance to once again experience her own culture filled her with joy. Such thoughts prompted her to share the songs that she loved with Freyja.

Her time with Freyja, even so, had brought new possibilities she had never before imagined. Freedom might mean staying as well as going and when she expressed this to Freyja, she saw a spark in her love's eyes.

Freyja had said nothing to put demands upon Fereshte, but had hoped she might choose to stay in the village, at least for a while to enjoy her new freedoms. Freyja remembered how her heart had fluttered as Fereshte's said she might indeed like to stay for a time. The memories only magnified the pain she now felt at the loss of Fereshte and the pain she felt for Fereshte's loss of her chance at freedom.

At the end of the night Freyja could see that Halig was weary. "I worry that you are not yet well enough for your work," Freyja spoke to Halig when he sat down to rest. "I do not want to leave you here alone."

"I still have two slaves to help," he coughed.

"But will they care for you and the Mead House?" Freyja asked.

Nora overheard and volunteered to stay. "Halig has many herbs for healing. I can use what he has and look for more to help him. I will stay." Freyja was relieved as she wanted to return to the predictable routine of the farm and the peace of her meadow. She needed time to mourn.

Brigit and Nora hugged a goodbye and Brigit walked to the farm with Freyja and Arndis. "Nora will do well for Halig. She is known as a healer in my father's house," Brigit said hopefully. Freyja did not answer. She craved quiet as much as the company of her family.

The animals were impatient to be milked and cared for so the women set about it. There was much bleating of goats, mooing of the cow, and the chickens were eager to be inside the barn. At first the noise grated on Freyja's nerves, but she knew that it was a normal part of the farm and was able to put it out of her mind. As soon as the women finished, they wordlessly hugged on the way to sleep.

Chapter Fourteen

Arndis looked for her daughter when she woke. She saw from the window, that the horse, cow, and goats had already been let out. When she went to the fire, she found a pail each of cow milk and goat milk. Seven eggs were in a pot so Arndis decided to boil them. Later she would halve them and remove the yolk, put mustard on the white, and replace the yolk. This was a favorite of Freyja's. Freyja must have been up early and Arndis understood that she wanted time alone.

Brigit came out to the fire. "I will do the milking," she offered.

"Freyja has done so. See," Arndis pointed to the bounty.

Brigit yawned and poured herself some milk. "I will see if Freyja wants to train with me," Brigit said.

Arndis shook her head, no. "I feel we should leave her for a time in peace."

Brigit nodded, "I will rebuild the signal fire. We have not done this yet." She took a small axe and walked toward the rocky prominence. She glanced toward the meadow to see a small smokey fire and Freyja sitting before it.

Freyja had heard a voice and woke early. *"Freyja do not despair. You will know 'inn matki munr', the mighty passion. There is lust, love, and the mighty passion. You will know them all and live a full and hopefully long life. You make your ancestors proud."* Freyja turned her head, started to look for the speaker, and then she knew the voice as her grandmother's. It had been too long since she had heard it. Perhaps she had not been listening.

She had been filled with energy when she awoke and wanted to get to her meadow. She took care of the animals and took their contributions to the meal fire. She hoped that might keep Brigit and Arndis in the house a bit longer.

Freyja went to her altar and brushed off dirt and pine needles. Her stone stood in a shadow and on the other side, the Brigit and Sven stones stood together. She looked at the small cedar and saw the fire ring. She would call upon Freyja. The goddess could fill her with warmth and a feeling of belonging. She hoped to feel this today.

She gathered wood and tinder then touched her flint to it. Eventually, a small fire blazed up. She added dried cedar and created smoke for cleansing. She stood over the fire and scooped her hands to pull the smoke up and over her head. She bathed in the smoke with the intention of purification. Then she sat cross legged upon the earth and brought an image of the goddess to mind. *"Freyja* of gold and lust, *Freyja* of dwarven lovers, *Freyja* of cat drawn chariot; be welcome at my fire, my heart, and my life. I light this fire to honor you. May the sweet fragrance please you. I bring you mead of quality from far away. I hope its golden color may please you. May its flavor warm and satisfy you." She paused after she placed a cup on the earth. Now that she invited the goddess, she should tell her why.

"I ask for your guidance. I had lust with Sven that was abandoned, friendship with Eric that turned into betrayal, and love with Fereshte that ended in death. Am I doomed in this? I do not want to love again." She sighed deeply and bowed her head with closed eyes.

She raised her pained face to the sky. "I did my best to fulfill the prophecy: 'When Freyja and Sven couple and children are born then we will trade with many and our village will prosper.' I should have worked harder to gain Sven's love. Perhaps we would have made it true. I could have made a child to start the prosperity." She listened to herself mumbling and feeling sorry for herself. This was not who she wanted to be.

"When the prophecy was changed, I did not know what to do. The Old One said, 'Freyja, will bring our village prosperity. And Sven, will bring us trade.' I believed that the ransom for Brigit would be good to bring prosperity, but now I know my sister and I do not want to lose her." Again, she hung her head and sighed. "I would call the ship back if I could. Her people might think her dead or sold into slavery," Freyja confessed.

"I sought guidance before and was sent to become a shield-maiden for the protection of my people. I prevailed with these skills, but lost love in the battle." Freyja let the tears she was holding back flow.

"*Enough, Freyja, you cannot speak so and be of my name. Why have you called me? To only whine and cry?*" The goddess would not indulge her.

Freyja felt like a child having a temper tantrum and pounded the dirt with her fists. "It is not fair that I have lost in every kind of love and still must bring prosperity. I do not know how. I am cursed. I am lost and lonely," she yelled at the goddess.

"*Do not beg for guidance, but find it in yourself. Listen and follow your intuition. I have given you my love and protection, now you must use these gifts. If not for yourself, then for your people. For the prophecy.*" In an instant, the fire was put out. It died in front of Freyja's eyes, leaving only coals to warm her face. Her wet tears seemed to give off steam from her skin. She looked around, disbelieving, in the silence.

Chapter Fifteen

Two days later Freyja took the horse to the village. She called to the Mead House before she dismounted. "Halig, I am here to carry out my duty to Fereshte." There was no hearty shout back in greeting. She went inside and let her eyes adjust, from the early morning light, to the relative darkness.

"Here, Freyja," Nora called out. She was seated on the floor next to Halig. "He is not as well today."

"Oh, by *Odin*, I am fine," Halig gritted his teeth and pushed with his legs. His back was against the wall so he slid up to standing. He leaned his weight against the wall, holding his side with one hand.

"I will go to Fereshte and gather her bones," said Freyja matter-of-factly.

"No, I shall come too." Halig reached out his hand to place it on Freyja's shoulder. She stepped close and put her shoulder under his arm. She glanced over at Nora with a question in her eyes. Nora shook her head, sadly.

Freyja helped Halig to the door. "Let us take your cart, Halig. That way if we collect things, we may bring them back," said Freyja lightly. Nora understood and went around back to bring the cart to the door. Freyja hitched her horse to the cart while Nora helped Halig up and inside. He did not argue about riding while the women walked.

Nora made light conversation. "We have had a few people come to drink wine. Many say they like our mead better," she laughed.

"Yes, my mead is always good," Halig spoke up now. "We have been trading for many roots and Nora has made good stews. The brothers of the forge bring chickens sometimes."

"I have made broth for Halig these nights to help with his fever," added Nora.

"Good broth, with herbs," Halig smiled and nodded while patting his stomach.

"We are near, Halig. Please tell us what to do. Nora will help me." They stopped the horse before the sand was too deep for the wheels of the cart to roll. They were next to the rocks dotted with sea grasses and could see the place where they had left Fereshte's body.

"You will gather her bones bravely, with no tears, for she is going to the next world. Her soul will be weighed worthy," he smiled slightly with memories behind his eyes. He pulled the sheepskin out from underneath himself and handed it to Freyja with some laboring.

Freyja held back her tears during the gruesome task. She and Nora gathered the torn shroud bits and bones among the rocks. Some were scattered, dry and sandy and others had some flesh still upon them. Freyja had seen death and wounds, but this was different. This had been Fereshte, her lover and close companion. Her skull had been removed from the body and was a bit away. Freyja and Nora both stood awhile, looking at it. Some of her beautiful black hair was strewn about. Left by the birds who did not take it for their nests or left by the sea winds which had carried most away. Freyja was breathing hard when she knelt to retrieve the skull.

She put both knees on the ground in a moment of weakness and stayed, transfixed. She rocked forward and back slightly and reached both hands to the skull. A loud sound pierced the silence. The gurgling croak of ravens. She followed the sound to see two ravens perched on the limb of a nearby spruce tree, watching. She raised the skull to them with both hands. "Tell *Odin* what we do this day. *Munin* and *Hugin*, say what you have seen. The body of a warrior dealt with, as is her custom, but no less honorable than our own. I will bury her with her sword. I ask that he accept her into *Valhalla*." The birds cocked their heads and watched.

Freyja stood and Nora held out the sheepskin to accept the skull along with the rest. Freyja took the bundle, turned her back to this place of sorrowful duty, and returned her friend to the cart. They turned the cart and walked toward the forest and village. The ravens followed beside them, resting in trees. After they had gone a bit, Halig spoke. "Now, find and dig a resting place for her bones. I see no harm in placing her sword with her. After all, she had become one of us in many ways." He smiled at Freyja.

Freyja carried the bundle into the forest. She and Nora used their knives and hands to dig in the soft loamy soil until they had a good trench dug. They lined it with the bits of shroud and placed the bones, not as a skeleton, but as a bunch. Her sword was placed to one side. The skull faced east, towards the rising sun. They reverently buried the remnants of their friend and covered the grave with stones. "*Odin*, keep her safe here and welcome her brave spirit to *Valhalla*," asked Freyja. She carved a rune of protection on a stick. She cut her finger to trace the symbol with her blood and staked the rune stick for *Algiz* into the ground. They heard the croaks of the ravens again as they emerged from the forest.

They returned to the cart to find Halig slumped over. "You are done?" he asked.

"Yes. She is ready for her journey to *Valhalla* and in a protected place," Freyja said as she climbed into the cart. She helped Halig lie down and held his head in her lap. Nora led the horse back to the Mead House. The two ravens flew a circle over the cart and then flew back toward the sea. Halig raised one hand to the sky. "*Odin* gives his blessing. He will hear that you have done well."

Nora ran to get Halig's slaves to carry him inside. When he was laid on a table, he let his shoulders relax down and Nora opened his shirt. His wound was festering. She cleaned it and made a poultice of herbs. She wrapped his torso in hopes of keeping the wound closed again. She had a wet cloth and was wiping his feverish brow. "He worked much yesterday and slept long. He would not let me check his wound before we left to Fereshte. Now this!" Nora was worried. Halig shivered and Freyja found a skin to cover him. "Build the fire," Nora instructed a slave. "Cold and hot. This is not good," she knitted her brows and bit her lip with worry.

"I will stay with you tonight," Freyja touched her shoulder.

Freyja had a slave care for her horse. She and Nora busied themselves working on the Mead House needs. They washed cups to ready for tomorrow and arranged the shelves to know what supplies they had. They found places to sleep taking turns to watch Halig. He called for water once. Another time he began to thrash about so the women moved him to the floor, near the fire. At the first rays of the sun, he cried out loudly. Freyja was sitting by him, her head fallen on her chest. She must have dozed off. Nora woke and ran to them. "What does he say?" she asked Freyja.

"He calls for his wife, dead these many years. He calls my grandfather's name and others who are also dead," Freyja whispered. "Perhaps he sees them." Halig reached up to Freyja wanting help to sit up. She and Nora each took an arm and sat him up.

"Freyja, Freyja you must ..."

"I am here, Halig. What do you wish?"

"Freyja, I wish you to have the Mead House. All of mine are dead as is Fereshte now. I have no one and it is a good life. Promise me you will keep it. The village needs it," Halig coughed up some frothy blood.

Freyja looked around as if someone could tell her what to do. She felt a deep prodding and was inspired. "Yes, I promise. I will keep the Mead House for you."

"You will need my two slaves and my chest to help you. This is good... Now bring me my sword. I will die with it in my hand, even if not in battle," Halig rasped. Nora knew which was his sword and hastily brought it. Freyja placed it in his hand and he smiled. "Yes, now I join the line of my people," Halig said and laid down. He began to sing, his voice growing quieter as he sang. Freyja sang along and he closed his eyes and smiled. At the end of the song he roused, opened his eyes, and shouted, "Mead." Nora ran to get some and brought the cup to his lips. He tasted of it then closed his eyes to take his last breath.

Nora and Freyja sat for a bit in quiet. "We will sleep and, in the morning get Halig his burial clothes," said Freyja. She took the cup from Nora's hand and drained it. She walked heavily to where the mead was kept and surveyed the stores, knowing that they would need it all on the seventh day. "But now, we drink to Halig." Freyja poured a cup for each of them. Mead for her, wine for Nora. They drank their cups, staring into the fire.

Chapter Sixteen

In the morning, they and the slaves spread the news of Halig's death. Several old women came to bathe the body under Nora's watch. Freyja walked to Og and Helga's nearby farm. Helga was known for the fine cloth that she and her slaves wove.

Freyja approached the doorway and called out, "Helga, I come to tell you news."

Helga came bustling out the door, wiping her hands on her apron. She recognized the voice and was prepared with a sour expression on her face. "What news have you, girl?"

"Halig has succumbed to his wound. We prepare him for *Valhalla*," Freyja spoke slowly.

"I am sorry to hear. We will miss him, but he will be welcomed by *Odin*. Why do you come? Why not send a slave?"

"I am seeking some of your fine cloth made into burial clothes for him," ventured Freyja.

"And so, I have something you want?" Helga said in a nasty tone, rubbing her hands together.

"Yes," Freyja decided to keep herself calm. "Your cloth is known to be well made and your household skills famed for garments." The flattery was working, bringing a slow smile to Helga's lips.

"Well now. We will make such fine clothes as you have seen for Halig. He left coin for such?"

"Of course," replied Freyja though she had not thought that far and would need to find out.

Helga turned around and began yelling orders to her household. "We bring them tonight and you will have silver and mead ready for us," she yelled over her shoulder to Freyja as she walked back into the house. Freyja could see her pointing and waving her arms.

When Freyja got to the Mead House, Klause had arrived with a troop of young men carrying axes. "We have come to build Halig's pyre," Klause said solemnly.

"You may take the cart for your use," Freyja answered gratefully. There were many parts to burial and she had not been thinking well. The boys put Klause's horse to the cart and began the hunt for wood. They would build the pyre just on the sand, away from the forest.

Freyja found Nora making stew at the fire. "Nora, we will need to pay silver for the burial clothes and mead. What do you know of Halig's wealth? He said he had a chest, but I have not seen it." Nora and Freyja began looking everywhere for a chest or pouch of silver. They moved every bag and bundle on the shelves. They reached behind crocks and bowls. They did discover pickled fish and cabbage. They found some fermented roots as well as hard cheese. Freyja remembered seeing barrels and bags being stored in Fereshte's loft so climbed the ladder. She swooned when she looked at the sleeping bench. She sat down and fingered the soft sheep skins. She had been thinking now of Halig and Fereshte had not been in her thoughts. She closed her eyes and let the bitter sorrow wash over her like waves. She felt herself dive under those waves and hold her breath. Two friends lost in such a short time.

She came up for air. Their village battle had been small in comparison to most. What must it be like to lose many in battle? Was she prepared to truly be a shield-maiden? She opened her eyes and looked before her. Bags, barrels, mostly empty filled the space. Something caught her eye. A sparkle at her feet. She bent down to look under the sleeping bench. A pair of shoes with threads of gold in them caught the light.

She knelt on the floor and lifted a skin. Under the bench was a chest. She pulled it out with effort and opened it. Many coins of silver, neck bands, and necklaces much like Helga's, filled the chest. There were goblets and some jewels. An armband of silver with a mermaid on it dazzled her eyes. Yes, this would be enough for burial clothes, drink, and feasting, and even a large inheritance for herself.

"Nora, it is well you stop looking. It is found," she called through tears. "Thank you Halig," she whispered to the sky. She knew these riches would not change the past, but it would change the future. She put a large handful of coins in an empty bag then pushed the chest back under the bench. She took the shoes with her and climbed down the ladder.

Nora's mouth fell open looking at the shoes. "What wonder are these?" she asked.

"I think perhaps these were shoes of Fereshte. They are not strong, but very beautiful," said Freyja in awe.

Just then the brothers of the forge came through the door. "We have been told of Halig," said Kofri. "Is there something we can do?"

"The cart is with the young men who build his pyre, but tomorrow will you take it to buy mead?" Freyja asked.

"That we can do," laughed Hallr. "We know much of mead. In fact, we come to drink to Halig." They slowly walked to view their friend's body. He was scrubbed clean and his beard oiled. He somehow looked younger than his years, wrapped as a baby.

"Halig we will send you on to glory. Save us a place in *Valhalla*," said Korfi putting his mouth close to Halig's ear.

"Yes, his burial clothes come this night. He will look fine for *Odin*," smiled Freyja.

"Old friend, we will miss you," sighed Hallr. He moved away to sit at the table where he and his brothers always sat and Kofri joined him in a moment. Freyja brought them mead and Nora brought them all stew. "It seems Nora and now you know of this place, Freyja. What did Halig say of the Mead House?" asked Hallr.

"He asked me to take it and keep it for the village," answered Freyja shaking her head. The brothers looked to Nora and she nodded her head. "I did not think of this for me. Was he right in choosing?"

"Halig must have heard from *Odin* to say such. Let us honor his choice," said Kofri. The brothers raised their cups to Freyja. "Hail Freyja, Halig's choice." Nora joined them, saying so, until their cups were empty and they slammed them down upon the table.

"Enough. Your cups are empty," said Freyja good naturedly. She took their cups then returned to the table with the full cups and brought the shoes.

"The dancing shoes of Fereshte," Hallr chortled. "When Halig brought her, he had her dance many nights for us. She was a beauty, but Halig let no man take her by force. She was as his own daughter, able to choose and under his protection."

"Hail Halig," roared Kofri. They all raised their cups to Halig once more.

It was almost sunset when Helga came. She stopped to touch Halig. "The finest linen for Halig," she proudly proclaimed. Her slaves carried them in and laid the burial clothes on a table.

Freyja gently fingered the workmanship and nodded in agreement. "Yes, these are pleasing to the gods and man. You will want your silver and your mead, Helga," Freyja nodded to Nora and she brought a full cup to Helga as she sat at the table. "For your slaves as well," said Freyja feeling magnanimous. She brought a cup for each of the two slaves who sat against a wall. They grinned from ear to ear. Helga made a clucking sound with her tongue, but said nothing more until she caught sight of the shoes. She sucked in her breath.

"What are these?" Helga asked.

"Dancing shoes, from far away," answered Hallr quickly. "Such as these grace beautiful women whose dancing ensnares men."

"Halig had these from his travels," said Freyja. "They are nothing."

Helga reached out a shaking hand to pick one up. She turned it to study the stitching and made sounds of approval. "I will have these with silver for payment," she said firmly.

"But," Freyja started to protest, the old brothers shook their heads. The bartering began. The brothers spoke highly of the shoes and their worth, but in the end, Freyja gave enough silver for the clothes, as well. Somehow, she felt that Fereshte would approve of Helga's joy in having them. Helga put on the shoes and stood to lift her skirts and admire them. With a look, she urged everyone to comment on them and left happily with shoes and silver in her hands.

"We will be to the burning and the feasting tomorrow," she said on her way out the door.

After she left, the boys returned with Klause. "We have built a pyre on the edge of the sand. It is good and will send Halig well to *Valhalla*," said Klause. Nora made sure each boy had some stew and mead in thanks. The old brothers were more than glad to be included in another round.

"Tell the people that tomorrow we send Halig to meet with *Odin* at sunset on the sand," Freyja told Klause and the boys as they left to their homes. The old brothers left also and Freyja was glad of the quiet.

"We must dress Halig now," Freyja told Nora. They began their task which was not easy. The two of them had to contend with the stiffening body, but they managed. "He looks fine for his sending," said Freyja. They both sat down on a bench near Halig and his table.

"He is to burn?" Nora asked.

"Yes, he is to the pyre tomorrow at sunset. The next day, we put his ashes in a jar and bury him with his sword," Freyja explained. She realized it must be hard for Nora to understand. She had become part of Fereshte's foreign burial, not of her choosing. Now she was a big part of Halig's.

Nora shook her head. "Where I live, most are buried in the earth. These are strange ways to me indeed."

"I thank you, Nora, for helping me. I have needed your help and you have worked very hard. I will reward you with silver from Halig."

Nora squirmed a bit self-consciously. "I am here, so I help. You are a good person, Freyja, and you have taken your sister and me into your family."

"I am truly not sure what happens next, Nora. I now have the Mead House and two slaves. Is this my path? What of my mother and the farm?"

"All will become clear, Freyja. Let us do first what we must," Nora nudged Freyja's shoulder with her own.

"You are right. Tomorrow morning, we send for mead, tomorrow night the pyre and of course drink. Then on the seventh day we feast and drink to Halig. After those days,

I will decide what to do next. Will you stay with me until then?" Freyja asked with pleading eyes.

"Yes," Nora answered reassuringly. "For now, I must sleep." She made her way to the fire and gathered some skins to sleep. Freyja climbed the ladder to the loft to sleep on the bench that had been Fereshte's place of resting. She closed her eyes and shut out the past days of hurt. She longed for real sleep without interruptions of disaster.

CHAPTER SEVENTEEN

Freyja woke to humming. Nora was busy downstairs cleaning cups and straightening up. The doors were all closed to keep the chill air out. She was singing and talking to Halig periodically. As Freyja climbed down the ladder, the old brothers came in with some eggs from their chickens. Nora put them in a pot to boil while they all had a cup of mead.

"Now this is good mead. Sweet enough, but not too much," said Kofri. "It came from the south village and brings its warmth." He shivered and stomped his feet.

"I ask you to buy mead from the farm of the twins today. Take the cart and my horse. See if you can buy all that they have. We will need it tonight after the pyre and then for the feast," Freyja instructed.

"We will," said Hallr. "You may trust us to barter well."

Freyja gave them a bag of silver coins. "Come back before the pyre, at sunset." They pealed and ate the eggs hot out of the pot and washed them down with mead. The brothers wiped their mouths with their sleeves and stood to leave. They stopped beside Halig and whispered to him before they left.

"Do I cook for tonight?" Nora asked.

"No, we will have only mead, so I will be thankful if the brothers bring much when they come back," answered Freyja.

"Then what shall we do this day?" Nora wondered.

"Let us see what may be bought for the feast," Freyja thought out loud. They gathered some bags and baskets and walked out into the village with their shawls tucked around them against the cool air. They talked with people asking what they might buy for the feast. One woman said they might buy cheese from her and also a goat. They ended up, once again, at Og's farm. One of the servant girls ran to get Helga from her bread making.

Helga looked surprised, "What do you do here? Do you not like the burial clothes?"

"They are indeed fine Helga and he wears them beautifully. I come to ask about a steer for the feast. Do you have such a beast?"

Helga looked Freyja up and down with squinted eyes. "I do, but it will cost silver."

"I can pay," Freyja held out three coins. "Can your servant bring it on feast day and butcher for me?" Freyja asked.

"Yes, two more coins," Helga held out her hands and Freyja placed the silver there. Nora watched with raised eyebrows, but kept quiet. They all knew Freyja was paying too much. It signaled that Halig had left an inheritance large enough to pay for a good feast. Helga nodded regally and turned away quickly to hide her smile. It was not quick enough and Freyja knew she had smoothed the way a bit between herself and Helga.

Freyja and Nora continued their walk back to the Mead House. A few people they saw raised their hand in greeting. Even when she had been the focus of the prophecy, people did not greet her such as she was the daughter of Arndis, a woman who made her living bedding men. She raised her hand, hesitantly, in return. Much had changed now that she had a sister of worth, her mother did not profit from her love making, and she had proven herself as a shield-maiden, a defender of her people. She felt and acknowledged these changes within herself. This realization was sudden and now in a peaceful moment, surprising. It made her glad of what she was doing for Halig and that the people would see this.

Klause and Sven saw them walking and joined them. Both had a new attitude of respect. Freyja thought that it was because they had fought, side by side. They had seen what each was capable of. "Are you ready for the pyre?" Klause asked them. Nora nodded.

"Halig is ready in his finery and thanks to you the pyre is ready. We wait for the brothers to bring mead and the people to gather at sunset," said Freyja.

Just then the brothers came down the path with a full cart. "Hail all," yelled Kofri. "The gods have aided us. We have mead and even some ale. The father made some last year and it is fine," he grinned broadly.

"The boy who is their slave now has proven to be a good climber and is bringing down plenty of honey for a next batch, so they sold us all but a small amount," added Hallr. The brothers were both a bit wobbly.

"I will help," offered Klause and Sven at the same moment. The brothers grinned and did not refuse the offer. Klause, Sven, Freyja, and Nora unloaded the cart while the brothers told stories. They laughed in the gathering twilight and tittered even more when they realized they could see their breath.

Soon the sun was low on the horizon and the people came wrapped in their cloaks and carrying their torches. Arndis and Brigit arrived. Brigit nodded to Sven in the crowd and made her way to him. They stood and spoke quietly of Halig. Helga and her household came with the Old One and her family. Karle's family was conspicuously absent.

Klause got the boys, who had helped build the pyre, to put Halig in the cart. He lay, looking honorable with both hands clasping his sword upon his chest. Helga came close to inspect his clothing and looked at Freyja approvingly. People walked toward the shore and the pyre talking softly, one to the other.

The boys, Klause, and several of the older men placed Halig atop the pyre and stepped back. The Old One approached to whisper words to Halig. She stepped back to loudly say, "*Odin* hear us. We send Halig to you. He has earned his place in *Valhalla* and we ask you to receive him in his place of honor." She motioned to some with torches to light the pyre. The boys had built it well and the flames leapt up quickly. She had brought runic symbols of protection carved on pieces of wood for his journey. She threw these into the fire saying the words to go with them.

The fire grew hot and the faces were bathed in the orange glow. The youngest faces showed awe and wonder at the huge fire with its greasy smoke. The old faces tipped to the sky with eyes following the smoke. The heat drove people back and they found that they had created a perfect circle around Halig on his pyre. Parts of the pyre fell in on itself as the intense heat brought down timber. Sparks flew into the darkness and fell harmlessly on the sand. People drew back further and mothers sat with children on their laps. Old ones found logs to sit on. The roar of the fire and the sound of the waves behind them made a sort of music in the night. The people felt bound to each other by the practice of their ways and comforted in knowing their place in the cosmos.

Hallr and Kofri helped the Old One up on the cart and turned it to go back to the Mead House. Others began to slowly follow, a few at a time, as the fire died down. Those who had been with Halig at his final battle stayed the longest; Sven, Brigit, and Freyja. Finally, Freyja broke the silence, "I will come tomorrow for his ash and sword. Now I am to the Mead House and the crowd," she sighed.

Her feet were heavy as she walked. Her skin prickled from the change of the hot fire to the cool evening. Tonight, she would serve mead. In a few days, she would host the feast and then her funeral duties would be over. What then? Become the Mead House owner? Cooking and serving. Cleaning and breaking up fights? She could not see it clearly as her future and she felt no joy at the prospect. As Nora had said, 'Let us do first what we must.' She put on the face of a good hostess and entered the throng. The warmth of the Mead House was stifling and the smell of humanity assaulted her nose. She left the door standing open.

"Here. Take these to Helga," Nora thrust three cups of mead in Freyja's hands. Nora turned quickly back to filling more cups. The old brothers had a group of boys around them, regaling them with their tales of life. One of the boys learned that he had been too gullible when Koffri could hold a straight face no longer.

"Old men and their lies," the boy grumbled as he went to join another table as Freyja passed by.

Freyja took the mead to Helga who was speaking to the women sitting around her. They hung on her every word. "She came to me for the burial clothes. Said my weaving was known for its fine quality. I was busy, but I did it for Halig," Helga spoke importantly.

"This is true," Freyja added to the conversation while she delivered the cups. All the women's faces looked shocked, mouths fell open, and Helga was beyond pleased. They all leaned in to listen to Helga more as Freyja left.

After everyone had gotten a drink, the Old One stood. She raised her cup. "We have sent Halig on and tonight we drink his inheritance mead, because of many. We thank the gods for accepting him into *Valhalla*. We thank Klause and the boys for building his pyre. We thank Brigit, Sven, and others for defending him when the village was raided. We thank Nora for caring for him in his last days. Finally, we thank Freyja for carrying on the Mead House as his heir." People looked around with each name and nodded at the person mentioned. When the Old One named Freyja as Halig's heir there were gasps followed by quiet.

Kofri stood, "And why not? She fought with him and she and Nora tended to his wounds and his burial."

Nora stood tall, "I heard it from his mouth. This is what Halig said."

Kofri's brother, Hallr, stood to join his brother and Nora, raising his cup. "Hail Freyja. Hail to the Mead House." Others joined in more enthusiastically as they realized that the Mead House would continue to be available to them.

Freyja raised her hands to calm them. "In Halig's name I give another cup to all. The rest we save for the feast!" There were cheers and more hails to Freyja and Halig.

The cups were again drained amicably and the people left for their homes. Arndis came to sit next to Freyja. "How is this for you, my daughter?" she asked waving her hand at the room.

"I am not sure. Nora has said we need only do now what we must. After the feast I will decide what to do."

"It could be a good way to make a living. Hard work and service to the village."

Freyja only shook her head. "I am glad of Nora's help," she said as Nora approached them.

"I am happy to help, though I miss you and the farm, Arndis."

"I miss you as well, Nora. Brigit helps me greatly. Where is that girl? It is time we go to care for the farm," added Arndis.

Arndis, Nora, and Freyja looked around the room to find only a few people still there. Brigit was sitting by the fire, quietly staring into the flames. Arndis stood and called to Brigit, "Brigit, we must to the farm. The animals are tired and so am I."

"I go with you now, Arndis." Brigit came to say goodbye to Nora and Freyja with hugs.

"Mother, please take the horse. I am sure he is missing the farm as I am. It will make the journey swifter." They all walked outside and watched as Brigit and Arndis rode off on the horse.

Nora and Freyja put an arm around each other's shoulders to look over the Mead House. There were cups to wash and skins to refill with mead. The floor needed sweeping and wood for the fire needed to be collected. The women's faces fell then they laughed together. "It was a good night. We will work tomorrow," Freyja said . Nora took one last cup of mead to sit by the fire. Freyja decided to join her.

"At the house of Brion we drank ale. Good ale, but I now prefer the warmth of mead. The ale makes me full of air while the mead fills me with sweetness," Nora stated . She realized that she was a little drunk and a little more than tired.

"I too like mead best, Nora," Freyja replied, raising her glass with a smile. "We are lucky the bees like our lands and share their honey with us."

"We have honey in the Far Isle, but do not make it into mead. It seems that the honey is more for the masters in their houses than the people," Nora mused.

"I'm sure it is different in other villages where they have jarls and such. Here we have only Og, our headman, to be fearful of," Freyja yawned.

"Og is to be feared?" asked Nora in disbelief. "I fear Helga more."

"And you are right to do so," Freyja laughed as she planted a good night kiss on Nora's cheek.

CHAPTER EIGHTEEN

The next day, Freyja took Nora with her to the pyre. They took a beautiful clay jar they had recently traded for and filled it with Halig's ashes. The fire had been intentionally made hot enough to burn bones and all. Freyja thought reverently about Halig and Nora was whispering in her language. When they were finished, they walked together to the waves without a word. Tiny bits of ice clung to the sand as if trying to establish a footing for the winter. They washed their hands and then the outside of the jar in the near frigid water. Freyja carried the jar back within the circle of her arms and Nora carried Halig's sword.

They stopped at the spot where they had buried Fereshte's bones and dug another pit nearby. The ground resisted in the cool of morning. "I think this is good," Nora said. "Friends should be near each other." Freyja smiled remembering some of the arguments that she had witnessed between them, but felt that it was so.

"Yes, it is good that they are near each other." She placed the jar in the pit and Nora laid the sword beside it. They covered the items with soil and then stones. "I will ask the

Old One to carve some runes on a stone that this place may be further protected," Freyja said as she stood. They both sighed as they looked at the two burial places and again felt the loss that the village had incurred during the raid.

For several days Freyja and Nora worked on the Mead House. Firewood was stocked, skins were filled with Mead, cups were washed, and the floor swept. Freyja found someone to repair the benches that had been broken in the raid on the village. The place looked very nice and ready for Halig's feast.

Only a small number of people came to the Mead House in the next days as few had coins. The old brothers had earned some from Freyja for getting the mead so came to spend their coin on that same mead. Helga brought a friend nightly and spent her own coin. She nodded at Freyja and spoke respectfully to both her and Nora. On the night before the feast, she reminded Freyja of her part in it. "I send my slave with the steer in the morning. He will butcher and help you with the cooking fire. You may have him for the day. At feast time I will bring bread, as I know how much you like it," said Helga magnanimously. Freyja could only nod enthusiastically, as she was so taken aback.

The feast morning was glorious with brilliant sunrise matching the colors of the newly turning leaves. Freyja felt the change in the air. The change to winter was slowly trying to get a foothold and settle in. The men would be coming back from the negotiation voyage soon. They would need to arrive before the ice started to build up. She said a quick prayer to the AllFather, asking that all would come back safely to their village and family. The changes to the village would be greatly noted by those returning. So much had happened during the summer.

Helga was true to her word and her slave was adept at butchering. All the steer was collected and used, then the animal spitted over the fire. Children had appeared to watch with interest. They begged for a bit of the blood to paint themselves and Freyja gave them a bowlful.

Nora was busy with cooking stew and dried fish was being made into soup. They had asked Arndis to bring butter and cheese and of course more roots, as they had brought on every visit. The farm was known for growing roots now, more than anything else. Freyja thought back on the days, more than a year ago now, when it had been known for the love making skills of her mother. Things had indeed changed and she thought it was for the better.

As the day unfolded, people came by with contributions to the feast. Food began to pile up on the tables. At dusk people began to arrive and the lamps were lit. The cooking fire and the gathering villagers began to warm the room so none noticed the early chill signaling the change of season.

All who entered greeted Freyja and hailed Halig. As the feasting began in earnest people took turns telling stories of Halig and singing songs to praise him. The feeling of the night was happy even though it was tinged with the losses of Halig and Fereshte. Others who had been wounded in the raid, were now healed. The new slaves had settled into their work and showed no overt signs of revolting.

The young slave at the twin's farm was even sweet on both girls and they flirted with him constantly. Their mother was now watching them all intently. Freyja wondered at their father's reaction when he returned with the ship, hopefully before the ice formed.

There were only a few minor scuffles during the night over this word or that word or an implied slight. A small fight broke out when Ivarr thought someone had taken his cup. He stood up to sing a song and as he was ready to sit, could not find his cup. Helga pulled it out from under him, just in time, as he began to sit on the bench. He had forgotten that he put it there.

"Oh, Ivarr. I was keeping it for you," Helga lied sweetly as she handed him the cup.

He grumbled a bit saying, "Women, being too helpful." Helga's intervention went against her reputation and everyone was impressed. She and a few others had kept the punches from flying. All was peaceful and no one was feeling the stresses of life in the moment.

Someone even brought up that the negotiators would soon return and perhaps bring more prosperity. At that Freyja and Brigit exchanged long sad looks. Freyja again wondered about her part in the unfolding of the new prophecy.

Younger children were falling asleep and mothers gathered them up after one more, "Hail, Halig." The older children were rousted by their parents, telling them they had work to do in the morning. The Old One and the old brothers were helped to their feet and tottered out after the Old One placed her hand on Freyja's head. "You are more than a farm girl, more than a shield-maiden. Your life will be long and good."

Once more Freyja and Nora looked around seeing much work to be done. "In the morning," they both said, smiling at each other.

Chapter Nineteen

The morning dawned crisp and bright. They felt the nearing of winter and the return of their men. The cool weather was invigorating and Freyja and Nora were both energized by it. Nora had built up the fire when Freyja climbed down from the loft. The women found much food untouched from the night before to eat as they worked on cleaning up. Helga had contributed great amounts of bread and some stew was left. The steer, however, had been eaten voraciously.

It was leisurely work and they did not hurry. Nora asked the two slaves to gather left over food and drink from plates, cup, and bowls into buckets to take to the pigs of Joarr's widow. The two piglets Freyja had gifted to her after the death of her husband were growing well.

"Stop at the old brothers and ask them to come here when you leave the widow. I would speak with them," Freyja asked.

By the time the slaves and the old brothers had returned, the Mead House was back to normal. Nora was stacking plates and bowls while Freyja swept the earthen floor. "Hail

Freyja and Nora. We sent Halig off well last night," yelled Kofri clapping his hands together.

"We did indeed," replied Freyja with a smile. "I am thankful for all who gathered."

"I hope you have called us to help with an open keg of mead," Hallr ventured. Nora had not waited for them to sit, but had filled cups for them already. As the brothers sat the mead appeared before them. "It is well that we are here. We will help as we can," Hallr raised his cup in salute and then to his lips.

The brothers sat with their cups and Nora and Freyja joined them. "It will be quiet again until the men return," said Kofri.

"Yes, that is what I wanted to talk about.," Freyja started. "I had a dream last night about the Mead House. People were talking and laughing around the outside while there was trading. It seemed to be market day and all had gathered."

"But market day is at the cross roads where the three roads meet, always," Nora spoke.

"That is the way, so that travelers who come and go may buy and sell," said Hallr.

"It has always been so, yes," said Freyja. "But what if it changed? It could be outside the Mead House and then people could come inside after."

"People always come here after a good day of trading," said Hallr with his hand upon his jaw. He nodded, "Such a dream seems an omen for prosperity from The Lady, herself."

"I have coin to have a smith build benches against the outside front and side walls for trade goods to be displayed," Freyja's voice took on an excited note.

"We pass by Ivarr's as we go back to our forge. We will tell him to talk with you." Kofri stood. He seemed eager to have a mission. "Come Hallr, we must go." Hallr quickly drained his cup and joined his brother at the back door. They both raised their hands in parting.

"This dream is true?" Nora asked Freyja.

"Yes, I saw it as if it were today and all the people seemed happy," Freyja replied.

"So, you will stay at the Mead House?" Nora made it sound like a statement rather than a question.

Freyja's mouth twisted and she bit her lower lip. "The Mead House must continue for Halig's honor, but I long for the farm. Nora, you now know much about it. Would you keep the Mead House for me?"

Nora laughed, "I? Remember that Brigit and I will go back to the Far Isle after the negotiations. We are not of the village." Freyja had almost forgotten. She had become close to both Nora and her half-sister, Brigit.

Freyja let out a huge sigh. "Well then, can you stay at the Mead House until then? Can you care for it in my name?" Freyja's eyes pleaded.

"Yes, I will do as you ask. The slaves will help, but I would also like to be with Brigit. She is almost like my child. She could help and learn also," Nora stated. Brigit had surprised Freyja before with her knowledge of hunting and war. Perhaps this work would suit her as well.

"Yes. In a day or two we will go to the farm to gather your things and Brigit. Thank you, Nora."

Ivarr arrived with the old brothers in tow. "You want benches?" Ivarr asked. "There is no more room here. What are you thinking?"

"No Ivarr, I have another idea," said Freyja.

"But first your mead," said Nora, bringing him a cup and winking at Freyja. Ivarr's face brightened and he tipped his cup and finished it off in several gulps. He wiped his mouth with the back of his hand.

"An idea?" Ivarr asked still standing.

"Yes. Come outside, in the front," Freyja motioned him to follow her. Outside she pointed to the walls. "You will build benches along the front and sides. My slaves will help you."

"Why do you need benches here? Do you want to give sleeping places to those who cannot walk home?" Ivarr laughed, pleased with his own joke.

"Oh, I did not think of such," Freyja joined him in laughing. "This will be a new place for market day trading. The benches will hold trade goods and the walls will block the wind and weather."

Now Ivarr was listening. He crossed his arms across his barrel chest. His lower lip stuck out while he surveyed the project. He paced the front and the sides of the building. "I will do it," he slapped his thigh with his hand. "We are rebels, you and I, Freyja. We think new thoughts."

"I give credit to The Lady as this idea came to me in a dream last night," Freyja said reverently.

"Then *Freyja, Vanadis,* guides you and I am pleased to help." Ivarr nodded with clear eyes. "I will take your slaves for the rest of the day," he said importantly. He walked through the front door, back inside, and held out his cup to Nora. She raised her eyebrows as she smiled and filled it. He motioned to the slaves to come with him. They looked to Freyja and she nodded her approval. The old brothers followed, always eager to see what was happening.

"The brothers look eager to have the company of men," Nora said.

"I am sure they miss Halig," said Freyja. "Most days will be quiet here, but we must be sure to tell all of our willingness to have market day here. Some may not want to walk further with their wares," mused Freyja with knitted brows.

"Yes, but they end up walking here most days after market. They will see," Nora said assuring her with a pat on her hand. "I believe you have followed the goddess' wisdom."

In two days' time, with much dust and noise, Ivarr had built the benches around both sides and the front of the Mead House. As he finished up, he showed off his work. "There is a bench and then there is a space. Like this all around. The space gives room for a person or an animal to stand," Ivarr exclaimed proudly. "Your men have helped greatly and should be rewarded. I will take some mead with my coin." He put out his hand.

Freyja smiled and took his hand in hers. She pulled him into the building and went to get both mead and coin, while he sat. "Here is mead for you and my men. You have done a fine job."

Ivarr raised his cup to the men who were more than pleased to be thanked and given mead in the middle of the day. "Now let us hope that it will be used come market day," said Ivarr.

"Will you tell all what you have done and that market is welcome to be here?" Freyja asked him while handing him his coins.

"I will. Now I am to home and family to show off my coins." He strolled out the door smiling, tossing the coins in his hand.

Chapter Twenty

F reyja told the slaves that no one was to come into the Mead House until night. They had the day to play games and relax. Nora and she began the walk to the farm. It was getting colder each day and they walked quickly to keep warm. "I will do my best at the Mead House, Freyja. I will honor you and Halig, both," said Nora.

"I know that you will Nora and you will be rewarded," Freyja spoke softly.

When they came in sight of the farm Brigit saw them and came running. "I have missed you so. Will you now stay?" The words tumbled out of her laughing mouth.

"We are again making changes Brigit, but all will be well," said Nora.

Arndis came down the steps wiping her hands, "What is this? I am happy to see you both," she hugged Freyja and then Nora. They all went inside by the fire.

"Nora is to keep the Mead House for me now. I am wanting our life on the farm," said Freyja.

"Oh?" said Arndis cautiously.

"Yes, she worked well with Halig and now myself. The slaves will help and she would like Brigit with her," said Freyja.

"The captives run the Mead House? This is most unusual," scoffed Arndis. She raised her eyebrows with an open mouth. She did not look at Nora or Brigit.

"I know, Mother. But they are no longer captives, but part of the village. Part of my family." She could see Arndis put her lips together and look down.

"Think how you now feel of these women," Freyja waved her hands toward the women and spoke more softly. "The village will accept it. Brigit fought alongside us to defend the village and Nora cared for Halig and then the Mead House with me."

"And you? Where will you be?" Arndis asked her eyes flashing.

"I will be here on the farm, with you," Freyja spoke gently. She realized that her mother needed reassuring.

Arndis' shoulders relaxed. "Ah, then. All may be well, with the help of the gods." Arndis stood hastily to get something so they would not see her worried face.

Arndis busied herself, handing out bread, butter, and goat cheese. She set out a good rabbit stew in their bowls. "The traps have been good almost every day," said Brigit between mouthfuls.

"I can see," Freyja said patting her back. Brigit had indeed filled out. "Hard work and good food serve you well." They ate their meal in comfortable silence.

"Do I go with Nora to the Mead House today?" asked Brigit.

"Yes, you will have some people come tonight as always and there is never lack of work to be done," replied Freyja in a business-like tone.

"Well then, I would show you some things before I go," Brigit pulled on Freyja's arm to get her to stand up. "Come."

Brigit pulled Freyja down the steps and towards the rabbit snares. "I have moved some as the bushes have grown. They are liking the grasses in the sun now as it is getting cooler." Brigit showed Freyja the changes she had made as they walked the line of snares. She reset two of them and seemed so adept, Freyja wondered that she had not grown up on the farm and in its woods. "Now, I want to show you the signal fire. I have rebuilt it. It is ready once again."

They turned back toward the farm and climbed the rocky prominence to reach the signal fire. "Brigit, this is very good. You have built it well my sister," admired Freyja.

"Thank you. I am glad it is well done," Brigit beamed.

Some trick of light caught Freyja's eye as she looked toward the sea. At the far south end of the fjord, she thought she saw smoke. "Brigit, do you see?" Brigit shielded her eyes with her hand. "There at the tip of the land. Is it smoke?" Freyja asked.

"Yes. I see it. Is it a signal fire? What does it mean?" Brigit's voice wavered.

"It may mean trouble or it may mean that our ship is coming back." Freyja's voice reflected the excitement and anticipation that she had felt as a child when she knew her grandfather's ship was returning. It had meant tales and treasures and special time with her grandfather who was sure to spoil her. Freyja turned to see Brigit looking down at her feet, her face clouded with worry. She suddenly remembered what the returning ship would mean to Brigit. Freyja took Brigit's hand in hers and knelt to look up in her eyes. "You are my sister. You will always be my sister. I will make sure that all is well for you. Do not worry." Freyja stood to hug Brigit. It took a minute for Brigit to hug her back.

"It will take two more days for them to reach the village. If it is our ship, they will sound the horn when they are near. If it is not our ship, I will light the signal fire. You must watch for it," Freyja instructed Brigit as they climbed down.

"How will you know?" asked Brigit.

"I know our sail from others," Freyja said as the girls raced to the farm house.

Arndis had helped Nora pack her things and had added some cheese, of course. "We have seen a ship," Brigit blurted out.

"I think it may be our ship returning," added Freyja. Nora and Arndis smiled and hugged each other like young girls, then stood patting each other's backs. "I thank the gods. I hope they return whole and well," Arndis spoke gratefully.

"Yes. I am longing to see Gunnar safely back," Nora enthused.

"Well then, now we have much to do as we wait for the ship. I will make ready for Tahir to stay at the farm," said Arndis happily.

"And I will look forward to seeing Gunnar in the village," said Nora, her cheeks flushing in anticipation.

Freyja interrupted this happy talk. "I have told Brigit that I will light the signal fire if it is not our ship. We will listen also for the horn, which our men will sound as they near the shore." Freyja turned seriously to Brigit and Nora, "You must tell all in the village of what we have seen. They must be ready for friend or foe. If it is indeed our ship, they must also be ready for feasting!" The last part was said with a smile.

In a few moments Brigit and Nora had their bundles gathered and began the walk back to the village. Brigit glanced nervously back, several times, at the farm. Freyja waved each time saying, "All will be well." Arndis' smile was not as broad, but she was now resigned to the new arrangement.

Freyja turned to Arndis. "Brigit worries about the return of the ship. I also. What will happen with the ransom negotiations? She will leave back to the Far Isle soon. I am not sure that is what she wants, in her heart."

Arndis looked hard at Freyja. "This is her life, Freyja. She is from another village and her people want her to return. The ransom will be paid to return her, not to have her stay in our village."

"I know, but she is my sister and now part of our life and our village," Freyja bit her lower lip and her eyes brimmed with tears. Arndis reached out to put an arm around her daughter and pull her close. They watched the women disappear down the path.

"We will see what the gods have in store for all of us, Freyja. Let us find some happiness." Arndis kissed the top of Freyja's head. "Now, we must care for the animals and the farm, if you have not forgotten how." Arndis laughed as she pushed Freyja gently toward the barn.

Chapter Twenty-One

T he next day flew by on the farm. Arndis wanted to air the beds, sweep the floors, and make ready for feasting. They made goat's milk cheese and butter from the cow's milk. They checked on their stores of food. Freyja brought several rabbits from her newly relocated snares and they started to roast them.

At mid-day Freyja climbed the prominence to search for the ship. She could see now that the ship was theirs, of the village. She heaved a sigh of relief. She had no desire to relive the invasion that they had suffered from Red Eric's ship on its second visit. There would indeed be much to tell the returning men of the time they had been gone.

She climbed down and entered the house to find her mother making the beds. "You will now have your bed back and I mine. They are ready," Arndis smiled widely with her hands on her hips. She looked satisfied and pleased.

"I will be glad to see Tahir also. It is good to see you smile with joy." Freyja mirrored her mother's smile.

"Oh yes. When we hear the horn, we should go to the village to take our food. Then we can go to the ship. The feast may be at Og's longhouse ..." Arndis' voice trailed off as she was planning in her head. Freyja just smiled and shook her head. The day continued much like the day before. They boiled eggs and made bread in preparation for the feast.

Arndis was shaking Freyja at first light. "Wake my daughter, we have a busy day ahead." Freyja stretched and tried to pull her mother into the bed. Arndis was strong, but Freyja stronger so Arndis ended up in the furs. Arndis made an angry face, but then started laughing. "You silly girl. Now, up," she swatted Freyja and crawled out of the bed. Arndis threw Freyja's shift at her to encourage dressing.

"I am getting up," Freyja laughed. She slipped her shift over her head and over her underdress then ran up behind her mother at the fire to tickle her.

Arndis squealed, "To your work, girl." Freyja danced down the steps to the barn. The goats and cow were milked and pails set outside. Eggs were gathered. Freyja joined her mother by the fire and they ate a *dagmal* of fresh milk and bread with butter. Freyja had put the horse out and he was enjoying some grass when the women were ready to go. They loaded bundles and baskets on the horse and began their walk to the village.

When they got to the Mead House, they pushed the door open to find Nora and Brigit eating and talking quietly. They had finished their morning chores and now were eating their *dagmal*. They had quickly embraced the morning practices of their adopted culture. Brigit stood to help them with their bundles, but Freyja motioned for her to sit.

"We will unload the horse and bring things in. You should eat, for we will have a busy day." Brigit nodded her thanks and sat quickly to focus on her food.

After unloading, Freyja and Arndis joined the others at their table. "I am glad you are here. I worry about today," said Brigit.

"Today will be filled with unloading the ship and feasting," said Arndis. "There will be no negotiations today. You will be busy with helping and have no time to worry." She patted Brigit's hand in a very business-like way.

"Negotiations will be another day with the Lawspeaker and the Old One," said Freyja. "We will be with you. Do not fear."

The door opened and two of Helga's slaves came in to buy two kegs of mead. Nora showed them and took coin from them. They rolled the kegs out the back door. "You are preparing the feast?" Freyja asked after them.

"Yes, Helga says after all gather here, that you will tell them to go to Og's longhouse for the feast," the shorter of the men answered.

"That is well," Freyja replied to the slaves. "I am glad of this," said Freyja to the others.

"I also," said Nora nodding. "We will have drink to serve and clean up, but feast cleaning will be for Helga."

"She has a large household and will be able," answered Arndis. "At least she will say that it is nothing." Helga had made life difficult for Arndis for many years and had only recently had any kind words for her or for Freyja.

At that moment they heard the long blow of a horn. They all startled a bit and then began to clean up from their meal. "I will hook the horse to the cart. We will help load from the ship," Freyja said.

"I will go with you so that I may see Gunnar/Tahir," Nora and Arndis said in unison. They both laughed at this and then all looked at Brigit.

"Go. I will stay here," said Brigit with a very small smile and a shake of her head.

The three women walked beside the cart toward the shore. A few people joined them and all chatted eagerly about the men's return. Soon they could see that the ship had put in south of Red Eric's sunken ship.

They had to stop the cart further away from the ship than they normally would, but they were sure the cart would be a welcome help. Nora saw Gunnar getting off the ship and ran to him waving her arms. His arms were full of weapons which he threw down when he saw her. "Nora. Fill these arms," Gunnar bellowed. He picked her up and whirled her around. There was great kissing and then he started loading her arms with items to take to the cart. As she turned away from him, he swatted her playfully on the butt.

Arndis looked for Tahir among the men, but did not see him at first. He was one of the last on the ship and he was holding on to Og. He helped Og over the side of the ship into the arms of a shield-maiden. When he followed over the side, he put Og's arm over his own shoulder. Arndis ran to Tahir and embraced him with one arm. "Well met, my sweetness," Tahir said warmly. "Let us help Og to the cart." Arndis could see that Og was wounded and his right arm looked to be tied to his chest under his cloak. Arndis walked on one side of Og with Tahir on the other side.

"Thank you," Og said to them both. He sounded tired. "Can I go home with you?" he asked Arndis.

"No, my friend. We are not friendly like that anymore," replied Arndis kindly. "Besides Helga waits for her warrior."

"Oh yes, my Helga," said Og as he was helped onto the cart. He lay down on his left side and relaxed in that position.

"He has been drinking mead. For the pain," said Tahir with a smile.

With the cart loaded, Tahir and Arndis walked hand in hand beside it. Nora and Gunnar came arm in arm behind. Freyja let go of the horse, as she knew it would go back to the Mead House, and turned back to the ship. People were telling stories about the ship of Red Eric and how it had come to be in the place where their ship would normally have tied up. Freyja noticed that of the last on board were three people who all wore dark cloaks with the hoods over their heads. Just like Brigit and Nora had worn upon their arrival. A feeling of apprehension washed over Freyja as she remembered what those cloaks had meant to her.

She stood and watched them climb off the ship. First a tall one, who then turned to help the others off. She approached them and motioned for them to follow the cart. They began walking and she followed. She could tell from behind that the shortest was a woman. The medium height and tall must be the male negotiators. Perhaps the woman was a servant sent to travel back with Brigit.

When they got to the Mead House, Og was helped inside by Tahir. Nora brought him a cup of mead then quickly began to help others. Arndis, Brigit, and Freyja all filled cups and delivered them to the ships' men. Family and friends began to arrive and the laughter and talking grew loud.

"Freyja," Nora yelled to get her attention. "Let us take cups to the negotiators." As they approached, the woman took off her hood and she and Nora both gasped in recognition. The woman stood to embrace her as Nora tried not to spill the cup.

"Nora," the woman cried in delight.

"Yes, yes," laughed Nora in both languages as she hugged her childhood friend. They talked and laughed. The tall man took a cup from Freyja and turned to join in the conversation. The other man reached for the cup in Freyja's hand while he removed his hood with the other. As their hands met, so did their eyes.

Freyja felt a bit uncomfortable as his eyes locked on hers, but she could not look away. It was as if she knew him, as if he could see into her soul, and he smiled. It was a slow, warm smile and she felt her face flush. She stammered something and turned. She felt his gaze on her as she walked away. Each time she looked over at him he was looking at her with soft eyes.

Helga came in with several of her servants. She looked for Og and bustled toward him with the air of an important headman's wife. Og stood when he saw her and bellowed,

"Helga, my love." He must have forgotten that his arm was painful for he reached out for her. She looked at his arm to see a blood-stained bandage where his hand should have been, and fainted.

Helga's servants got her on a bench and held a cup to her lips. She took a sip and was revived. She opened her eyes to find Og weaving in front of her. "Did not the Old One say that Tahir was to be my right arm?" slurred Og while laughing and holding up his arm. "Well, he has been indeed." Helga sat up and began to cry while talking to Og. Finally, she told him that the feast was waiting at their longhouse. Og stood and waved his bandaged stump. Yelling to the crowd he proclaimed, "My Helga has prepared a feast for us returning warriors. Let us go to enjoy her food and thank the gods for our return. Hail Helga!" There was a roar and the village began to walk to Og's farm.

"Oh Og, tell me of your misfortune," Helga asked. "What has happened to leave you as such?"

"Later my love. Let us enjoy the night." Og put his arm around Helga and leaned on her as they walked.

She looked concerned, but strangely happy. "Perhaps I should call you *Tyr*, for now you are like the fearless warrior god," she snuggled into him.

Tahir and Arndis walked, again arm in arm. Nora had Gunnar in one hand and her friend in the other. Freyja was left to escort the two men from the Far Isle and the man with the lovely smile never took his eyes off of her.

The feasting went on and on. The tales, the toasts, the singing lasted long into the night. Finally, Arndis came to Freyja, "Tahir and I will take the horse back to the farm."

Gunnar and Nora came to her as well. "I will take Gunnar with me to the Mead House," said Nora smiling. They stumbled out the door happily. Freyja could not find Brigit anywhere. She decided to walk back to the farm later as the crowd thinned.

Nora's friend spoke to her as she left, "We are to stay with Og's household," she motioned to include the cloaked men.

"Fine," nodded Freyja. "That is good." She was a bit confused as to why she would be told about where they stayed. Perhaps they knew she owned the Mead House. She left to have a quiet walk to the farm. 'Well, the men are back. The Mead House will prosper. Nora and Brigit will run it until … The negotiations may take them, take my sister, Brigit, away,' she thought. It was too much to think about and the mead had numbed her mind a bit. She walked on.

When she got to the farm she did not want to go to bed. She walked to her meadow and altar. There on the altar were the stones representing Brigit and Sven, side by side. Her stone stood to the other edge. It did not feel right to leave it there, so she picked it up and walked with it to her little fire ring. She built a small fire and sat with her stone in her lap. "*Freyja*, goddess. I call on you to guide me further. Continue your protection of me. You have guided me to prosperity through the Mead House and I thank you." She sat quietly and felt the love of the goddess wrap around her. Her eyes closed.

The dream again, in *Sessrumnir*. She was the goddess, seated at the head of the table. The doors were open wide. In walked Halig and Fereshte, laughing. Her heart gladdened and she hailed them. "Hail Halig and Fereshte, we are well met. Join me." They came to sit next to her and each kissed her on the mouth, in turn. They ate and drank together. They sang, told jokes and stories.

"We are happy here in *Valhalla* and happy to be in your hall. You must go now," said Fereshte holding Freyja's arm.

"But this is my hall. You are here, so now I will stay with you, my love."

"No," interrupted Halig. "You have more to do for your people. You are to fulfill the prophecy. Take our gifts and use them." Halig and Fereshte each took one of Freyja's arms and walked her to the door. They hugged her and stepped back to close the large and heavy doors.

Freyja's head jerked and she realized that she had fallen asleep at her fire. She decided to build up the fire and make a sleeping place for herself. Being near her fire felt comforting though she slept fitfully, hearing the voices of Fereshte and Halig loudly encouraging her. She woke up at sunrise with the vision of that man's eyes floating before her. They were rimmed with dark lashes and brows which set off eyes the color of the early spring grasses. They were so unusual; she could not get them out of her mind.

She pushed her arm into the soft ground to sit up and shook her head. She plainly heard her grandmother's voice, *"Keep listening for guidance from The Lady, Freyja, Vanadis. She and I will lead you to the mighty passion, inn matki munr."*

Freyja walked to the barn and woke up enough to milk the cow and the goats. She hugged the horse gratefully. and felt his steadfast friendship. The animals were happy to be let out to harvest the early dew from the grasses they nibbled. She smiled at them and carried the buckets into the house where she left them on her way, finally, to bed.

Chapter Twenty-Two

F reyja slept late and woke to find Tahir and Arndis outside by the well. Tahir was cleaning and sharpening his weapons. He had found Freyja's as well and was working on them. Arndis was playing with the goats as she kept them from the garden.

"Good day, Freyja. The feast was a good welcome back," said Tahir. "The men seemed to enjoy themselves and the mead was good."

"Yes," said Freyja. "The mead came from the next farm. They have made much even after their father left with you."

"Ha, yes! I hear they have a new slave who is good with their honey and the bees, thanks to you," laughed Tahir.

His voice grew serious, "I am saddened that Red Eric betrayed the village and his crew returned to do more damage. May he rot."

"You may be sure he rots in *Hel*. He did not go to *Valhalla* as I kept the sword from his hand after I cut his throat," Freyja said with a bitter tone. Tahir's eyes widened, his face showing surprise. This was news as well to Arndis who turned quickly to look at Freyja. "Yes, I killed Red Eric before he could force himself upon Fereshte. It is true."

"I am sad for your losses, Freyja. I knew you held him dear," said Tahir thoughtfully.

"It is no matter, now," Freyja said bitterly. She reached out to test the edge on her sword. "This is fine, Tahir. I will be ready for the next time my sword is needed. I just hope it is not with these negotiators. It would be a shame to put out the light in those green eyes."

"What do you speak of?" Arndis looked confused. Freyja did not respond, but hefted her sword, grabbed her axe, and walked toward the training place. She took out months of aggression and frustration on the stick men until she was covered in sweat and the tears flowed. She cried for Sven, Red Eric, Fereshte, and Halig. She cried for the father she had never known and the grandparents who had left too early. She cried for the years she had been bound to the prophecy and for the confusion she now faced in fulfilling it. She cried in worry over losing the sister she had just gained. When she felt drained of all tears, she dropped her weapons and fell to her knees. She raised her bare palms to the heavens.

She felt the sky darken and the rain fall on her in a sudden cloud burst. She started laughing and raised her head to feel the rain on her face. She heard the goddess laugh with her, *"Do not ask the questions, listen for the answers."* Freyja laughed and stood with her arms round her body, giving herself a hug. She rocked herself back and forth and let all her worries wash away. Freyja could hear Arndis squeal and Tahir laugh as they gathered the weapons and hurried inside. She ran for the barn.

The barn was filled with good memories of her animals over the years. It was also filled with memories of times with Sven and what she thought was love. Now she could see that it was only the prophecy that had moved her to lust. She had known lust with Sven and learned about her body and his. Only after she had let the first prophecy and Sven go, had she learned about love.

She lay down on her back in the hay and pulled a kid to her chest. It bleated softly and snuggled into her. She said a silent, Thank You, to the gods and goddesses for all the love she had known with Fereshte. She felt she must even be thankful for the time she had spent with Red Eric. She had learned even more about sex and love and the giving of her trust.

Chapter Twenty-Three

They were called to the Mead House to meet with the negotiators, the Lawspeaker, and the Old One. Nora and Brigit set the cups, full of mead, on the tables. Freyja, Arndis, and Tahir walked from the farm to bear witness and most of the village was there. Og and Helga were there as Headman and wife to lend authority.

The Old One stepped forward when all had assembled. "I call upon the wights of this place. Those seen and unseen. We ask you to be with us and protect us. I call the ancestors whose blood still sings within us to give us wisdom in this negotiation. Hail to all gods, *Aesir* and *Vanir*. Welcome and Hail to all." She was seated on the tall chair.

Gunnar told the assembled about the three who had arrived from the Far Isle; the woman who was a servant and friend of Nora's, the tall man who was a servant as well, and the man with the brilliant green eyes. "These three are from the House of Brion, father of Brigit," he started. "They come to negotiate her release with ransom and to return her, with them to Ireland."

Og looked to the free man, with the beautiful eyes, to begin the negotiations. He answered Og's nod by standing.

"I have been welcomed with your hospitality. I have put away my sword and will obey the decision of this village. I negotiate for the release of Brigit, daughter of Brion. I was told that Brigit was cared for safely. Nora has shielded her and the village has looked after her needs. Og has also told me that it had been decreed that; 'no harm will befall her; no man will lay hands upon her'. Is this true?" the green-eyed man asked of Brigit who was standing near.

Brigit answered with lowered eyes, "Yes, no harm has come to me," and she sat down quickly. She smiled a little too broadly. Her hand crept slowly forward and rested upon her belly.

"Of course. We have insisted," replied Og. "She has lived with her sister safely."

The green-eyed man looked puzzled. "What do you say?" he asked of Og. "Her sister, another woman like her?"

Og answered, "No. Her sister, also daughter of Brion. He also was our captive years ago. He made a daughter with Arndis, who is called Freyja." Og raised his good hand to signal to Freyja to stand. Freyja stood and the green-eyed man looked at her. His jaw dropped and he was speechless for a long moment.

"I knew Brion and was with him when he died. I grew up in his service and he was as kindred. That is why I wanted to see his daughter safely returned. I have sworn..." his voice trailed off.

"What have you to offer?" Og interrupted.

"I bring two chests of silver."

"This is a fair start," said Og. "And what more?"

The haggling began in earnest and many turned to their cups to leave the negotiations to the parties involved. Nora and Freyja were called to fill cups and visited with the people. Late in the night, people began to leave and the negotiations continued.

Freyja went to sit near the fire and listen. At this point, the two servants had been added to the two chests of silver. Nora spoke up, "I will take the place of my friend, for I now love this place. She may return to her home." Arndis threw her arms about her friend in gladness and Gunnar howled with pleasure.

The negotiator wanted to leave in the next few days, but Og refused. "The seas will be too rough and the weather unpredictable. We wait for the snow to melt and ice to break, as usual, for our travels. We travel and raid in summer. In winter we stay warm with our beautiful women." He winked at Helga. "You will stay with us and travel as we do. You will be well cared for." Og reached for Helga to help him stand. "It is ended for now," Og said and looked to the Old One. She had fallen asleep so Freyja nudged her foot. She roused to close the evening.

"Gods, we thank you for bearing witness. Ancestors, we thank you for attending this place. *Landvaettir* and *husvaettir* thank you for sharing this place and your protection." All raised the last of their cups, drank, and then poured the last into the offering bowl at the foot of her chair. She motioned Freyja to take it out to the base of a tree as she was helped down and into the arms of her family. "You may continue your negotiations as long as needed. When it is final, call me and the Lawspeaker again, to bless it."

The people left. Arndis and Tahir to the farm, Nora and Gunnar to the loft. The two servants followed Og's household to their farm. Freyja sat by the fire as it quieted. "I am called, Ian," a confident voice sounded over her shoulder. "I have sworn to Brion to always protect his daughter. Now I find there are two." He sat beside her and stared into the fire. "I can see you are of Brion. You have his eyes and are tall, like his people." He looked into her robin's egg blue eyes and she fell into the meadow grass of his. They held her for long and she had to shake her head to let go of the entrancement.

"Og will be wanting you. You should go," Freyja managed to stammer as she stood. She walked to the door and held it open for him. He brushed by her and she could smell the wood smoke in his hair mixed with his own aroma. His eyes caught hers once more. They stood eye to eye for a long moment before he smiled shyly, then walked out into the cool of the night.

She pushed the door closed and leaned her back against it. "What is this? Who is this? Why do his eyes hold me?' she wondered to herself. She closed her eyes and let his scent take her to a waking dream. They lay naked on a pile of skins on the soft loam of a forest floor. His aroma came to her nose mixed with the scents of earth and trees. It was a calming and grounding smell. Close by was a large fire which flickered and sent a shadow pattern dancing on their naked bodies. She could not tell if the warmth she felt was from the fire or their bodies. The vision felt so real she shivered and had to take a steadying breath. She shook her head to clear the vision and her jaw tightened. She chastised herself, "These are crazy thoughts. You know nothing of him. He is a foreigner. No more," she whispered.

CHAPTER TWENTY-FOUR

N ora climbed down from the loft to find Freyja and Brigit at the fire cooking bread. "Is Gunnar here?" she asked.

Freyja handed her warm bread and pointed to the butter. "Not here. Perhaps he is hunting." Nora shrugged and took the bread. She sat to visit about last night's negotiation. "I am so happy you will stay with us," Freyja smiled. "I want you to keep the Mead House for me and I want also to keep our friendship." Nora smiled. Brigit looked down at her fingers in her lap.

They did not see Gunnar because he had walked to Og's farm. He knocked on the door and a servant opened it. "I would speak with Og," Gunnar said. The servant turned and Gunnar followed to find Og at the fire with Helga.

"Gunnar, we are well met. We spent much time together. Do you still need to be near me?" Og laughed.

"Og, I have come to buy Nora from your service," Gunnar looked very serious.

"What do you mean? Nora? she is not of mine," Og responded quizzically.

Gunnar continued, "In negotiations you asked for the two servants and Nora offered to trade herself for the Far Isle woman. She is therefore now your servant."

"Yes, so it would seem," Og nodded, taking in the information. "And what will you do with Nora?" Og wiggled his eyebrows suggestively.

"I will make her a free woman and marry her." Helga made a face with knitted brows and left the room while Og thought.

Og put out his left hand, palm up, and waited. "So, we will call this her "bride-price" as if I am her family *fastnandi*, negotiator. I like this." Gunnar put some coins in Og's hand. He hefted the coins and jerked his chin up. Gunnar added a coin just as Helga came back into the room. She carried a bundle in her arms and put it down to walk up to Og. She reached out her hand and waited. Og sighed and handed her the coins, "It is the way of wives. You will see."

Helga put the coins into a beautiful cloth pouch and uncharacteristically handed it to Gunnar. "This is to be Nora's dowry and I give a new underdress, as well for your morning gift to her the day after the wedding." Helga hugged Gunnar and pressed the bundle into his arms. "Now you will have time to prepare the month of mead and your Frigga's day wedding."

Og smiled and shook his head, "Ah, so Helga helps in love. You must be back to your woman. May the gods protect you," Og stood as he clapped Gunnar on the back.

Gunnar almost ran back to the Mead House and burst through the door laughing out loud. "Nora," he bellowed.

Nora peeked in the back door. Gunnar strode quickly to her. "Be my wife."

"What? You are mad. How have you come to this idea?" Nora laughed.

"Say, Yes, and I will tell you," Gunnar grinned. He pulled her to a bench and sat her down to hurriedly tell the story of his visit to Og's farm before she could answer. He handed her the pouch and the bundle, all the while laughing.

"Yes, yes, yes," Nora replied and Freyja crept out the door and motioned to Brigit to come with her, to give them some privacy. Outside, they sat on one of the new benches. People would be coming soon to begin market day. They could hear approaching chatter. "Now, Nora will have the help of Gunnar at the Mead House. There will be a wedding," Freyja smiled eagerly at Brigit. Brigit just nodded quietly with a weak smile. "I am glad you can also help Nora while I go to the farm. In a day Nora has gone from a captive, to a slave, and soon a wife," Freyja hugged Brigit. Brigit's face seemed to hold many emotions and Freyja wished she knew what to say.

People started setting up their trade goods on the benches. There were furs, nuts, apples, and of course dried fish, salt, butter, and cheese. Brigit was distracted from her thoughts, helping people choose benches. The old brothers came with daggers to display and the spears that they made together with Tahir. She visited with them until Sven showed up at her elbow. Brigit looked into his face, burst into tears, and ran off. Sven's face fell and he looked around as if to find help. Freyja looked at him with one hand on her hip, the other shooing him to follow. He understood that and ran after Brigit.

Freyja looked over the trades and visited with buyers and sellers. Helga, Og, and their household arrived with some of Helga's clothing to trade. She smiled at Freyja, "I have given Nora a dowry. The Mead House must give her the feast."

Freyja smiled her most charming smile, "I have heard of your generous gift. I will gladly give the feast when it is time."

Helga pushed another woman's trade over on a bench to sit down and spread her clothing on her lap. "You see how fine the weaving is? Experience and care are shown in these clothes," she said to a traveler as she held up a shirt. Helga was no longer interested in talking to Freyja, so Freyja left her.

The trading wound down and Freyja had spent some coin on two furs. She said her goodbyes to Nora and Gunnar who were busy serving mead, each wearing a dreamy smile. She hefted the large bundle and started for the farm. She thought about how life might unfold there now. There had been so many changes to the farm in only one year.

She knew Arndis and Tahir would fill the farm with their love and she was happy for them. She also looked forward to getting more training from Tahir. There would be the winter and then they would send Brigit back to the Far Isle with Ian and the servant woman. She still felt conflicted about losing her sister. She would pray to the AllFather and the goddess *Freyja* for guidance and peace.

She heard quick steps behind her and flung her furs to the ground, turning with her sword drawn. "Ah," a man's voice yelled as he put his hands up. "I am friend. I come to help you." It was Ian.

"Then you should hail yourself as such." Freyja sheathed her sword in disgust. "You will be no help, if you get yourself killed," Freyja said, shaking her head. She bent down to pick up a fur just as he did also. Once again, their eyes met. An unusual sensation began in her breast. It was a mixture of excitement and panic. She could not look away, but felt uncomfortable.

Ian reached for her arm to help her stand. He picked up the other fur and dusted it off. "I will help you," he said and began walking.

She took a deep gulp of air and realized that she had been holding her breath. "If you must," Freyja said annoyed.

They walked in silence, but every time Freyja looked at Ian, he was already looking at her. His face lit up with a smile when their eyes met. As the sun was setting, he walked closer. Freyja looked at him with a scowl as he stepped closer. "Without the sun, I must come closer to the light," he said. Freyja rolled her eyes.

When they got to the farm Freyja said, "Thank you." She hoped he would go, but he took both furs in his arms and carried them into the house. Freyja came behind him and shut the door.

"Oh Freyja, my daughter, you are here," Arndis called cheerfully. "And who is this?" Tahir nodded to Ian in greeting.

"Mother, you know he is the negotiator. Sent for Brigit," Freyja said with exasperation.

"Come to the fire. We will have our *nattmal* and you will join us," Arndis patted a bench for Ian to sit.

The meal was good and Freyja realized that she had missed her mother's cooking. She ate heartily and found Ian watching her often. She self-consciously wiped her mouth with the back of her hand and sat up straight. "You must surely go to Og's and there is not much light left," Freyja said to Ian.

Ian stretched out his legs. "Og says that I am free to go where I want unless we meet to negotiate. I have all the winter to learn of your village and lands," Ian replied. Freyja's eyebrows knitted as she thought of what to say.

"Then you shall stay here tonight," Arndis interjected. "These furs will serve you well for sleeping by the fire," she smiled as she shook out the furs. Freyja made a face at her mother and shook her head, no, but quickly feigned a smile when Ian turned from Arndis to her.

"Well then, I am to my bed," Freyja said quickly and left the fire.

Ian's eyes followed as she left and Arndis brought him back to his senses. "You are welcome here. Good night, sleep well."

"Thank you for your hospitality," Ian said as he lay back in the furs and put his hands behind his head. He went to sleep with a smile.

Freyja tried to sneak by him in the morning, but he was not in the furs. He had found the axe and was outside, chopping wood. Freyja nodded at him. He smiled, put down the axe, and followed her to the barn. When she took a pail and milked a goat, he did the same. When she looked for eggs, he did as well. She looked at him with suspicion and he only smiled more. She did not like the conflicted feelings within her. She was annoyed having him in her space. She was happy for his help. She felt uncomfortable with his smiling.

She poured both pails of goat milk together and began to milk the cow. Ian stood and watched. When she picked up her pail, he picked up the other and followed her to the house. When they entered Arndis exclaimed, "Oh, thank you for your help, Ian. I am sure Freyja has valued it," she smiled at Ian and then at Freyja. Her wide-eyed look told Freyja to say something.

"I thank you for your help," Freyja said begrudgingly. Freyja put eggs in a bowl and Ian was reminded that he had some in the crook of his arm. He took a quick step toward Freyja as she stepped back and the eggs in his arm were crushed against her. Ian laughed nervously, with surprise as he pulled in his arm to contain the gooey eggs. Freyja lifted her apron dress to keep the goo off the floor and growled at him as she rushed to the well. Ian followed.

Arndis kept her laughter in until they were out the door then doubled over. Tahir came into the room to find tears streaming down her face and she gasped to explain what had happened. He smiled even though he could not quite understand her. Her laughter was catching. When Arndis finally caught her breath, Tahir understood what was funny. He smiled broadly, his teeth gleaming white, against his warm dark complexion.

At the well, Freyja drew a bucket of water and plunged her hands in to wash them off. She splashed some water on her apron. When she turned to put her hands in the water again, they met with Ian's hands, already in the bucket. He laughed and their eyes met. She wanted to be angry with him and frowned. Wanted to punish him for being so clumsy and for... smiling so much. Instead, she fell once again under the spell of his eyes. They were soft and warm and held no hint of judgement. They invited her to be happy with him and she felt herself begin to smile. In a moment she was laughing and splashing water on his arm to help clean it. Ian laughed, relieved that he had been forgiven.

Freyja shook her head, "There may be yet some eggs for eating."

"I will go without, for my clumsiness," Ian offered while pouring out the bucket. Freyja reached out to wring the water out of his sleeve and he widened his eyes, looking surprised and touched.

"Will you join us for *dagmal*?" she asked over her shoulder as she walked up the steps.

"Thank you, yes," Ian said, following her inside.

Arndis did not say anything about the eggs and placed some warm bread in each of their hands. "I have heard that you can do magic with eggs," Tahir said with a laugh. Freyja looked at him with one eyebrow raised. "You can make them disappear!" Tahir laughed at his own joke.

Ian smiled, "Yes, it seems this is true." He sat on a bench and Freyja came to sit next to him. It felt right to her, there was an energy between them, and she was happy.

"The cheese is very good," Ian remarked after Arndis passed some out.

"Yes, Arndis is well known for the cheese she makes from the goat milk," stated Tahir.

Ian looked long and hard at Arndis. "Arndis is a name I have heard before. I was raised in the household of Brion and he spoke often of you and his time on your farm." Arndis took a breath and adjusted her hair. "It is strange that his daughter ended up as a captive, once again on this farm."

"Yes, Brigit has been very welcome here. At first, we did not know that she was the daughter of Brion, sister of Freyja," Arndis motioned toward her daughter. "Now she is as one of our village and one with our lands," said Arndis.

Freyja looked down at her bread, "I had hoped that the negotiations would fail and she would stay here. Perhaps Og will decide that you have offered too little."

"Her brother desires her home. The family needs her and her promised marriage will benefit the family with trade and alliances," Ian said in a practical way. "She will leave with me when the ice breaks as we have negotiated."

Freyja felt the need to let out some emotions. "I will train with Tahir now. You must leave," she said to Ian.

"As you wish," Ian rose and turned to leave. "May I come again?"

Freyja replied a bit cooly, "As you wish."

Ian walked down the path while Freyja put on her sword in addition to the dagger she already wore. She did not wait for Tahir, but went to the stick men and attacked them. She slashed and she stabbed. She felt frustration at losing her sister, at gaining the Mead House, at these crazy attentions of Ian.

Ian had not gone far, but had stopped behind the barn to watch. He marveled at her form and strength. She had taken down her apron dress to her waist to free her shoulders and her sculpted arms maneuvered the sword with grace as the sleeves of her underdress billowed with the movement and caressed her skin. The fabric began to cling to her as the sweat appeared between her breasts.

Her body was beautiful, even in the anger that surely drove her. It was passion that was displayed and he suddenly realized that he wanted to be the object of such passion, in love. He had felt an uncanny attraction before and now it was intensified to passionate longing.

He closed his eyes, trying to slow his breath and leaned his shoulder against the barn. He could not appear as a love sick boy to these people. He knew he would have to regain his composure to return to the village and command respect as a negotiator. He lifted his chin and took in a slow, deep breath.

He felt the dagger at his neck before he heard anything. Freyja had crept to the barn when she had seen movement out of the corner of her eye.

"By the gods, it is me, Freyja," Ian choked out. He did not move, but kept his chin lifted.

"So it is," she panted.

OG'S HALL **VILLAGE**

MEAD HOUS

TWIN'S FAMILY

MEADOW

FARM OF ARNDIS

SIGNAL FIRE

SPRING

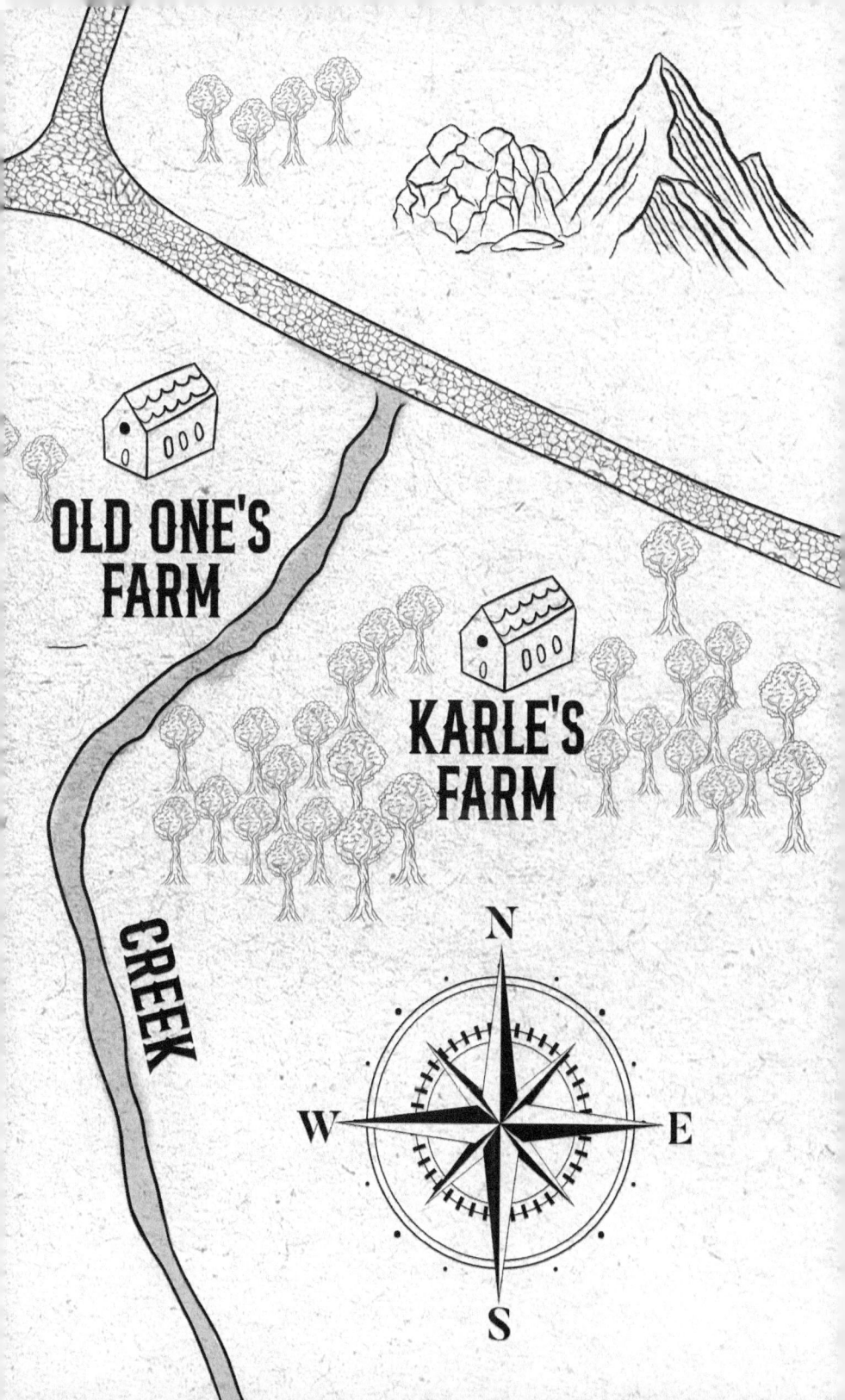

My Norse Prophecy fictional stories are inspired by Norse Pagan Gods/Goddesses and the traditions shared are those of the Viking Age. I have taken some license with variations of Germanic, Scandinavian, and Icelandic Pagan/Heathenism. My hope is that you will be encouraged to learn more for yourself through reading and research. My caution is that you be aware of groups and sources that may promote hate.

These stories are not intended to endorse White Supremacy, Supremacist or Nazi beliefs or practices. The travels of Viking Age Norse peoples took them around the world. They learned and borrowed from diverse cultures, especially through trade and intermarriage, thereby enriching their own culture. They sometimes settled in other parts of the world and brought their beliefs and culture to their adopted lands, as in the case of the Rus. Cultural diffusion was alive and well in those early times.

"Odin is the AllFather,
not the Some Father!"

Thanks to the historians and archeologists who work to improve our knowledge of the archeologic record of the Viking Age. Many thanks to Dr. Jackson Crawford and The Viking Answer Lady for cultural information of the Norse peoples. Tremendous thanks to my Beta Readers for their sharp eyes and even sharper tongues!